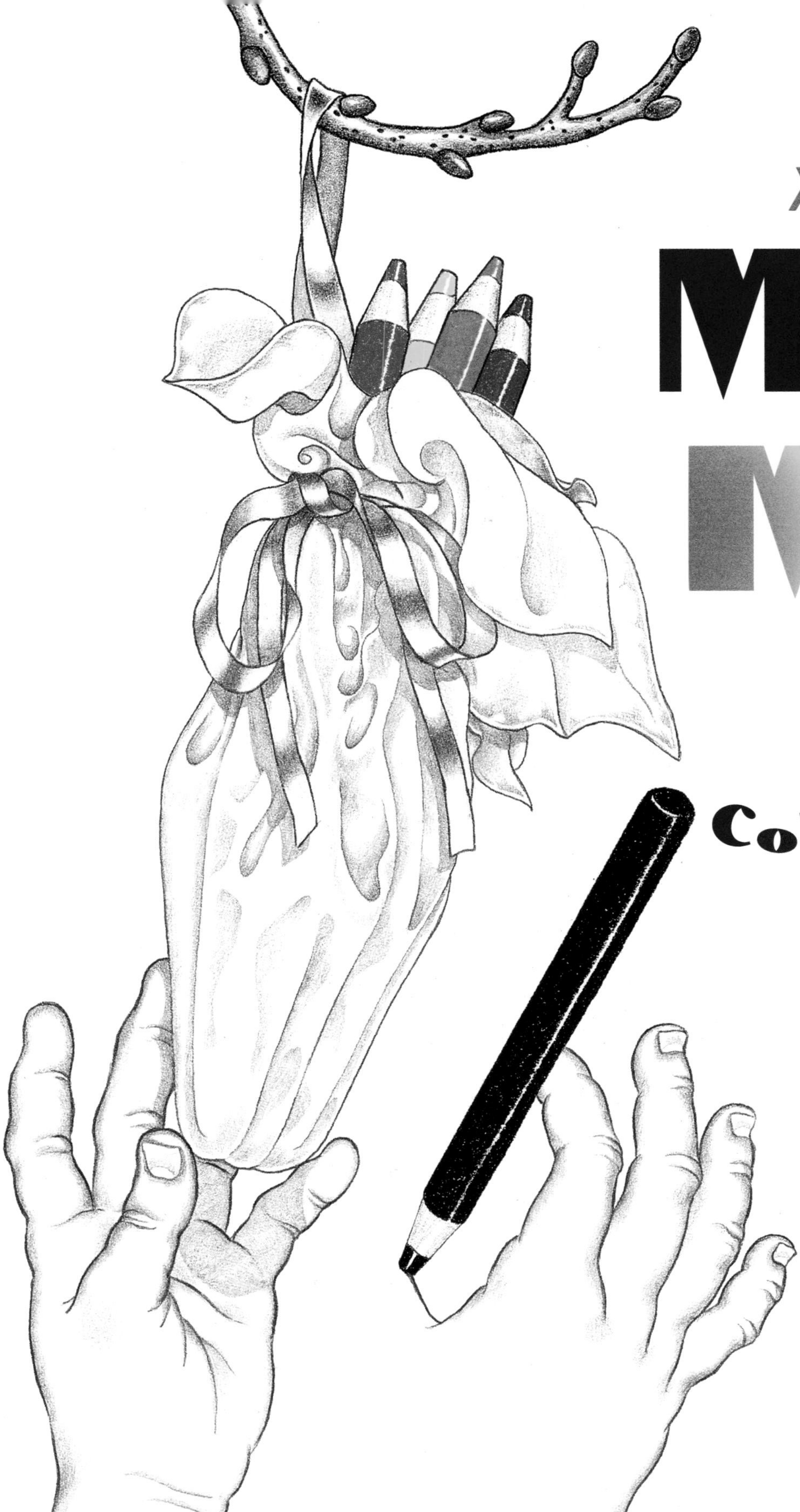

April Wilson's

Magpie Magic

A Tale of Colorful Mischief

Dial Books for Young Readers
New York

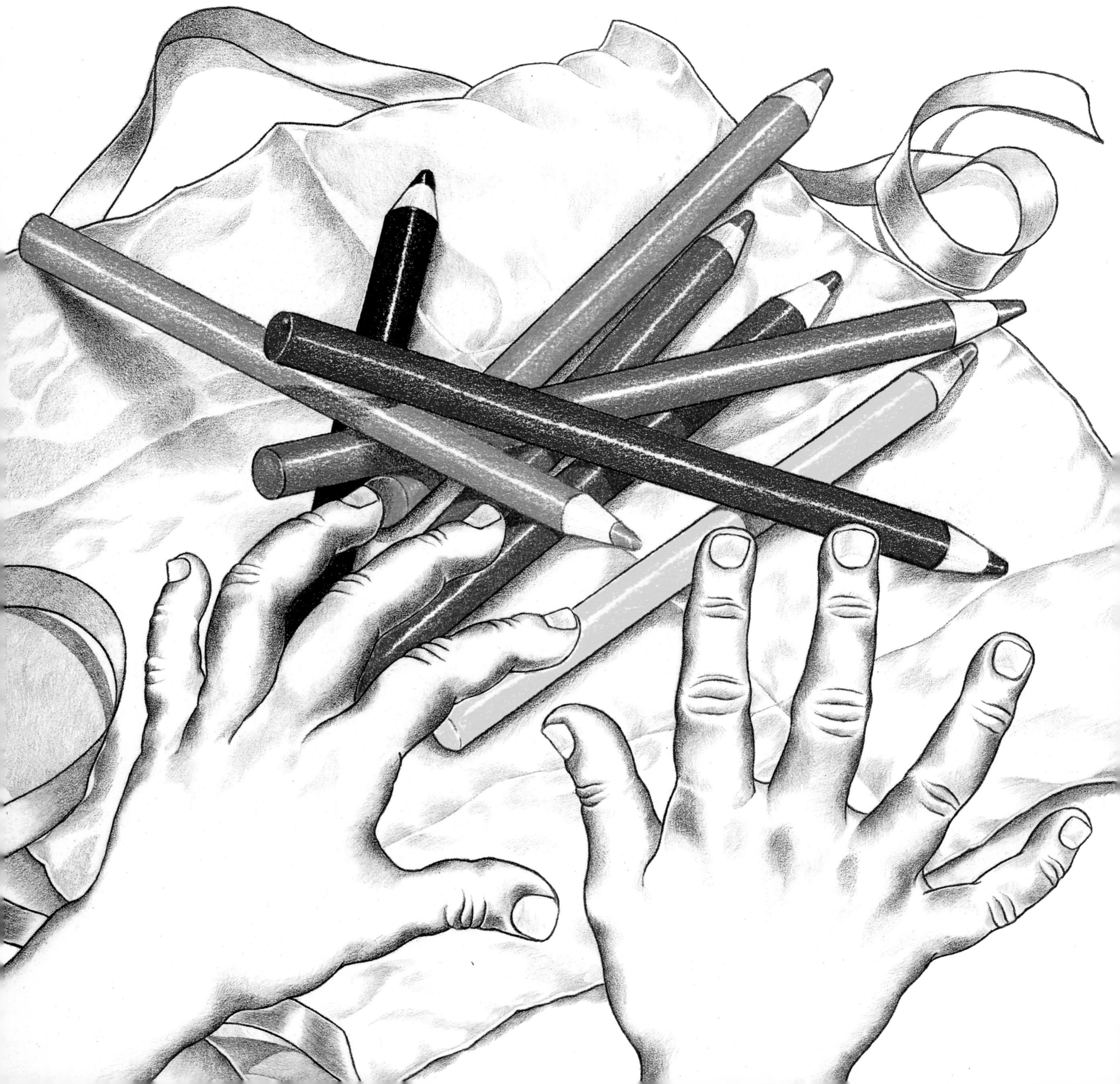

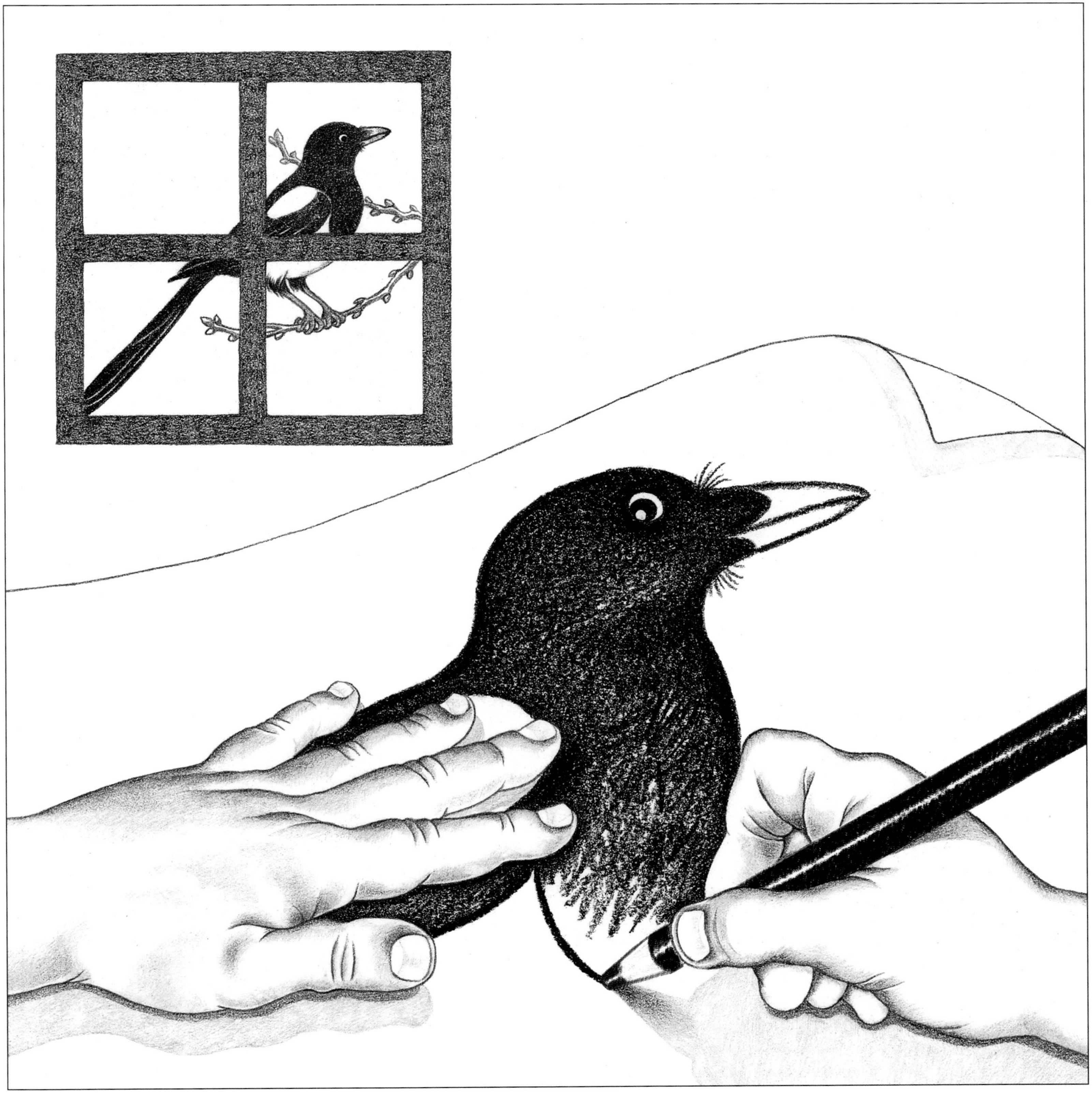

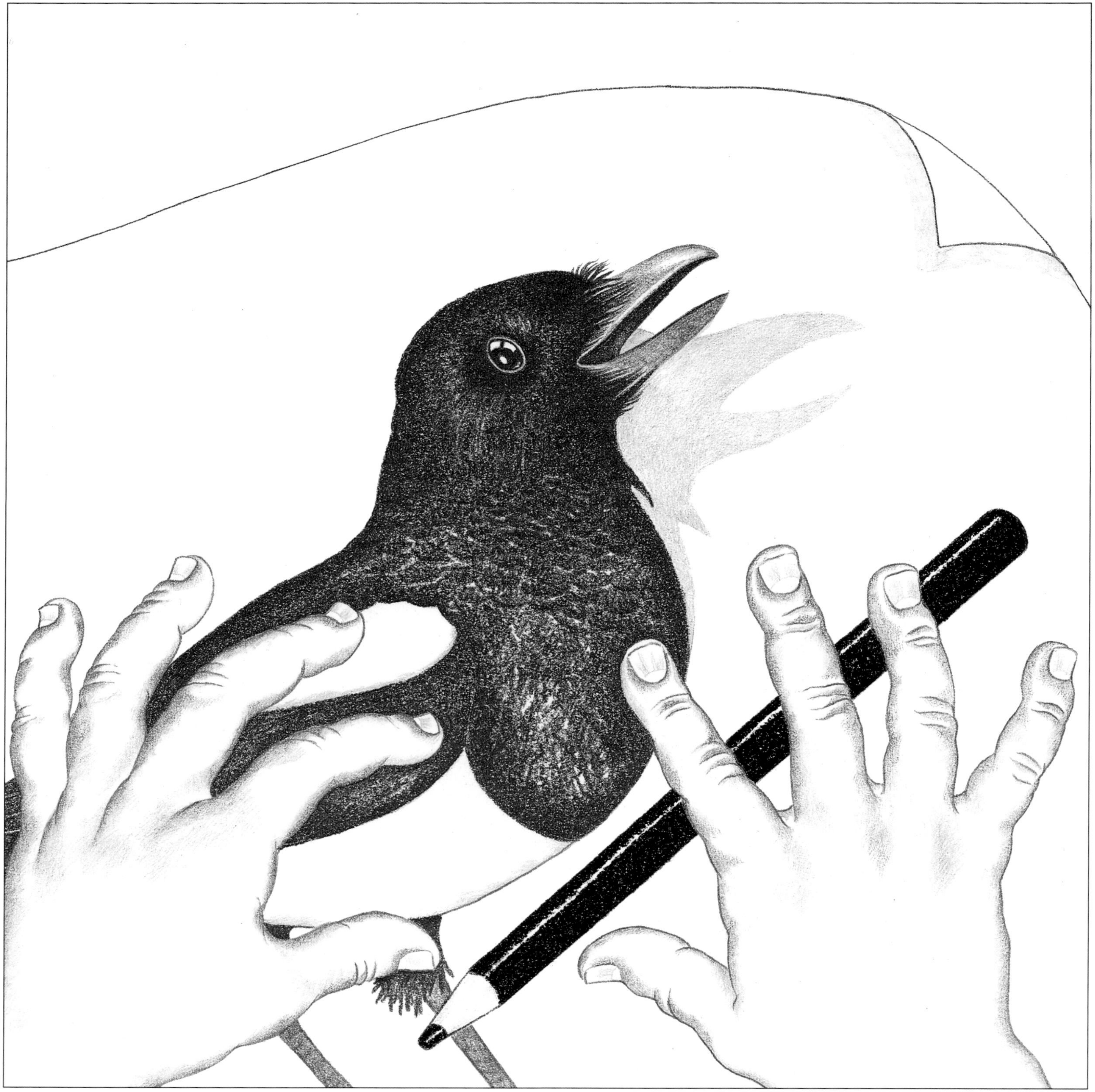

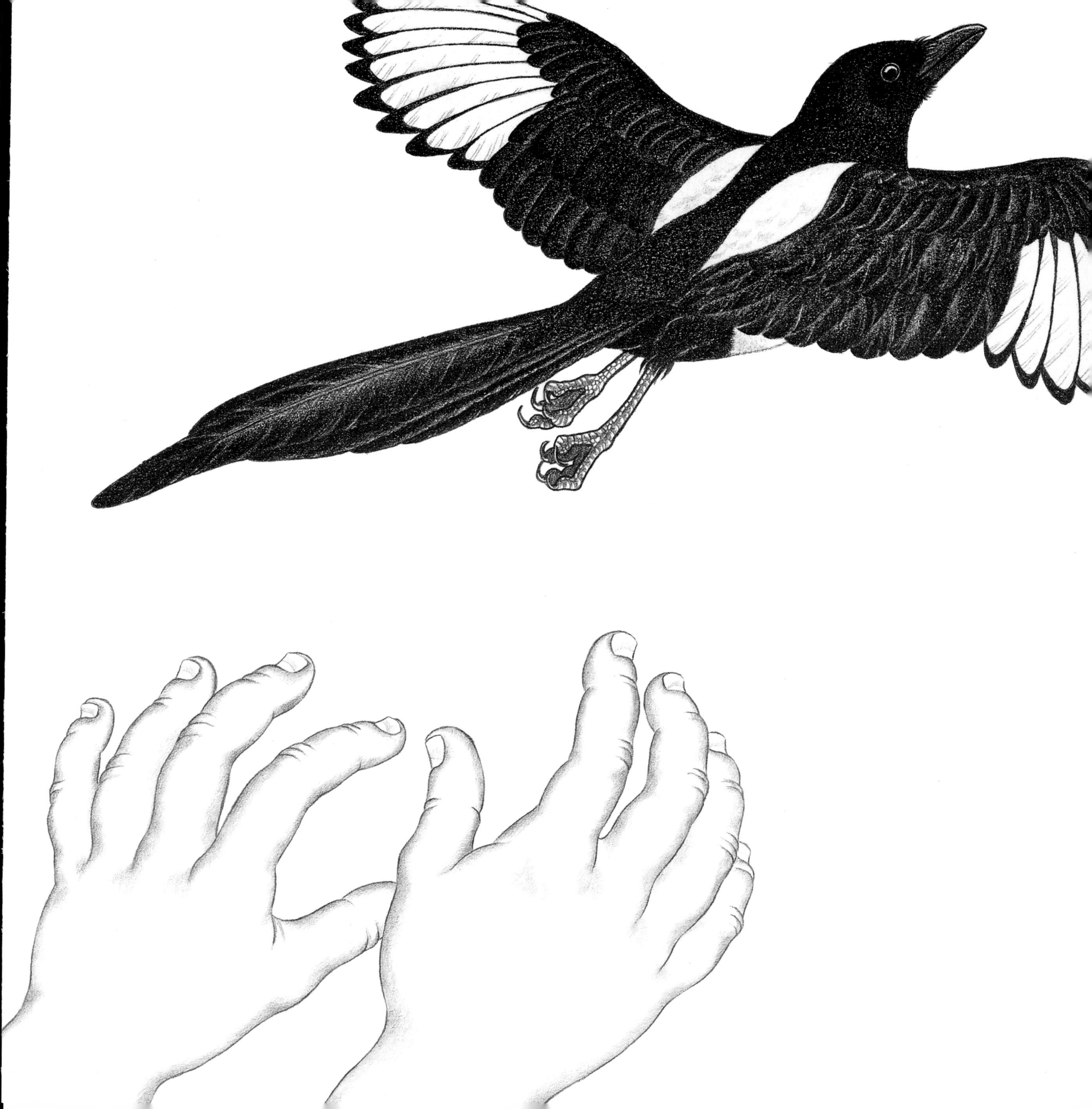

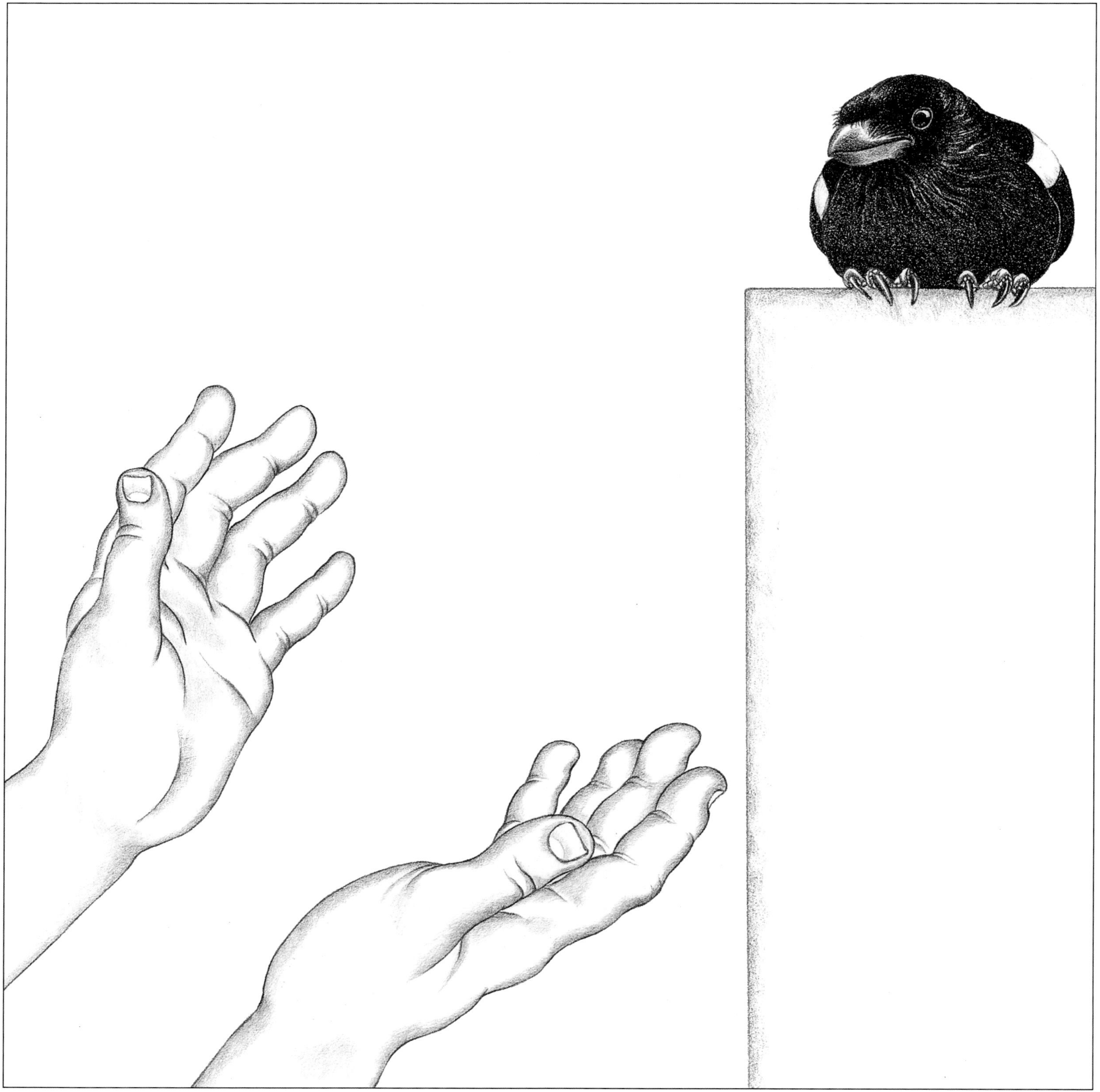

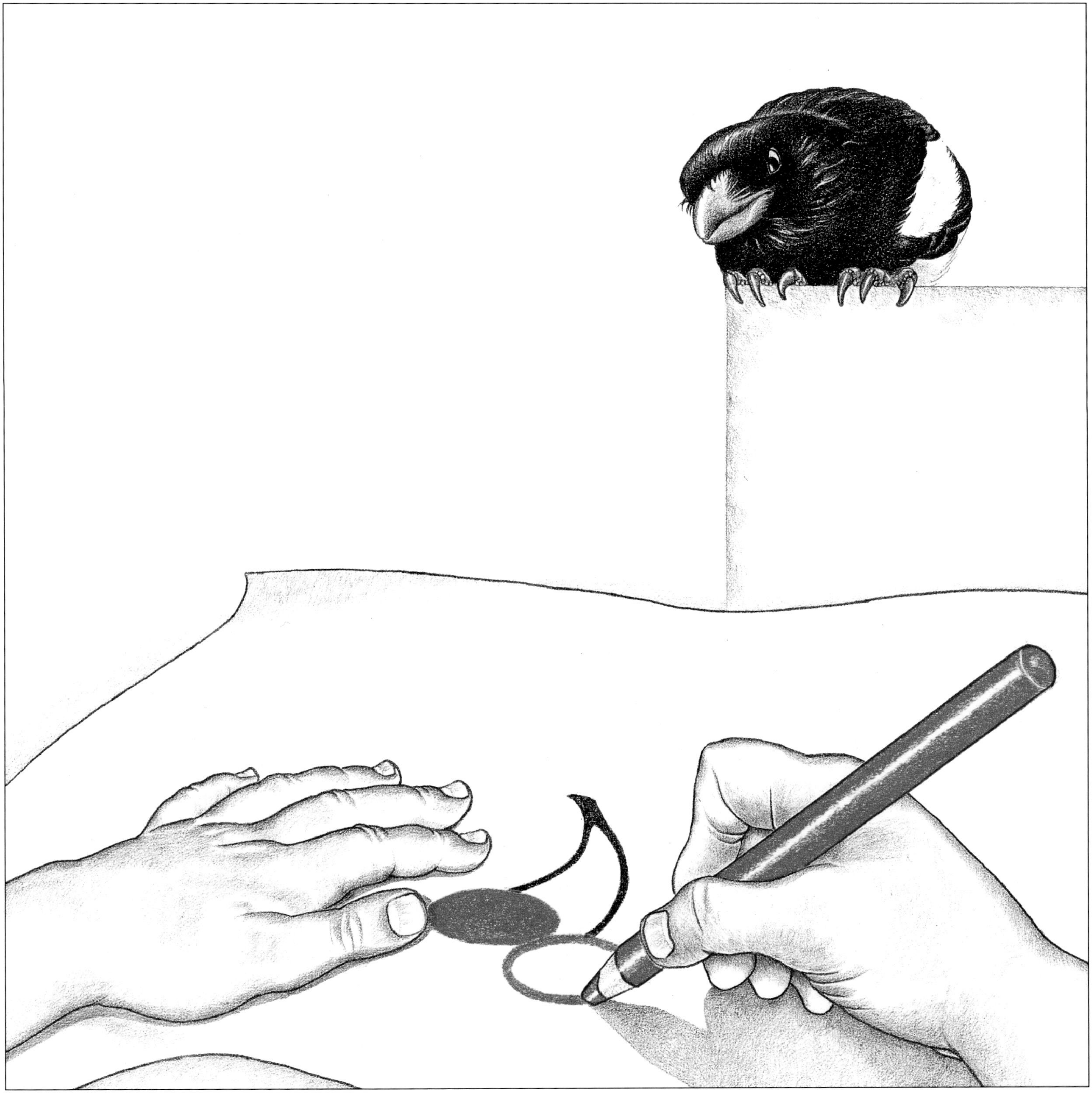

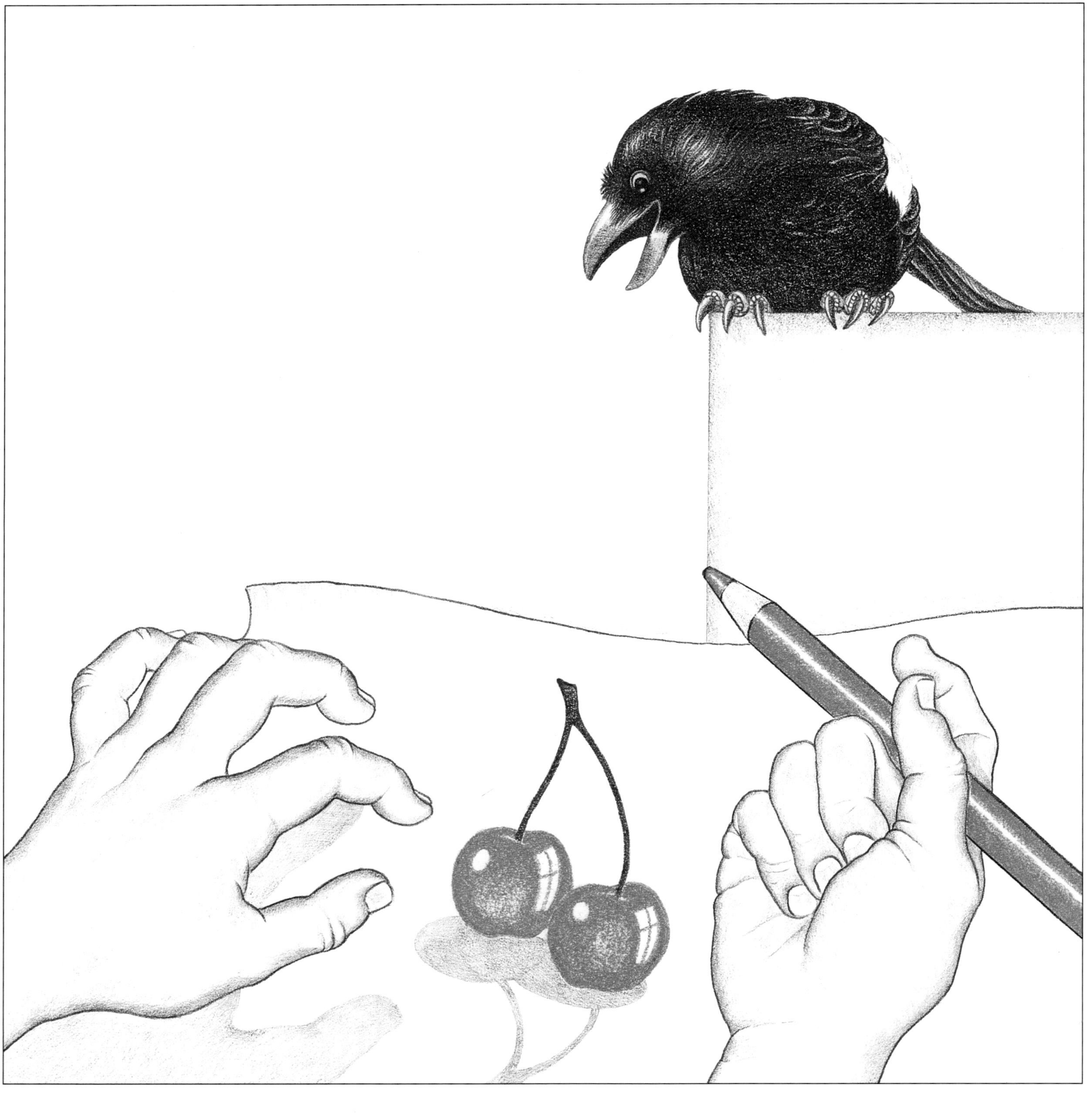

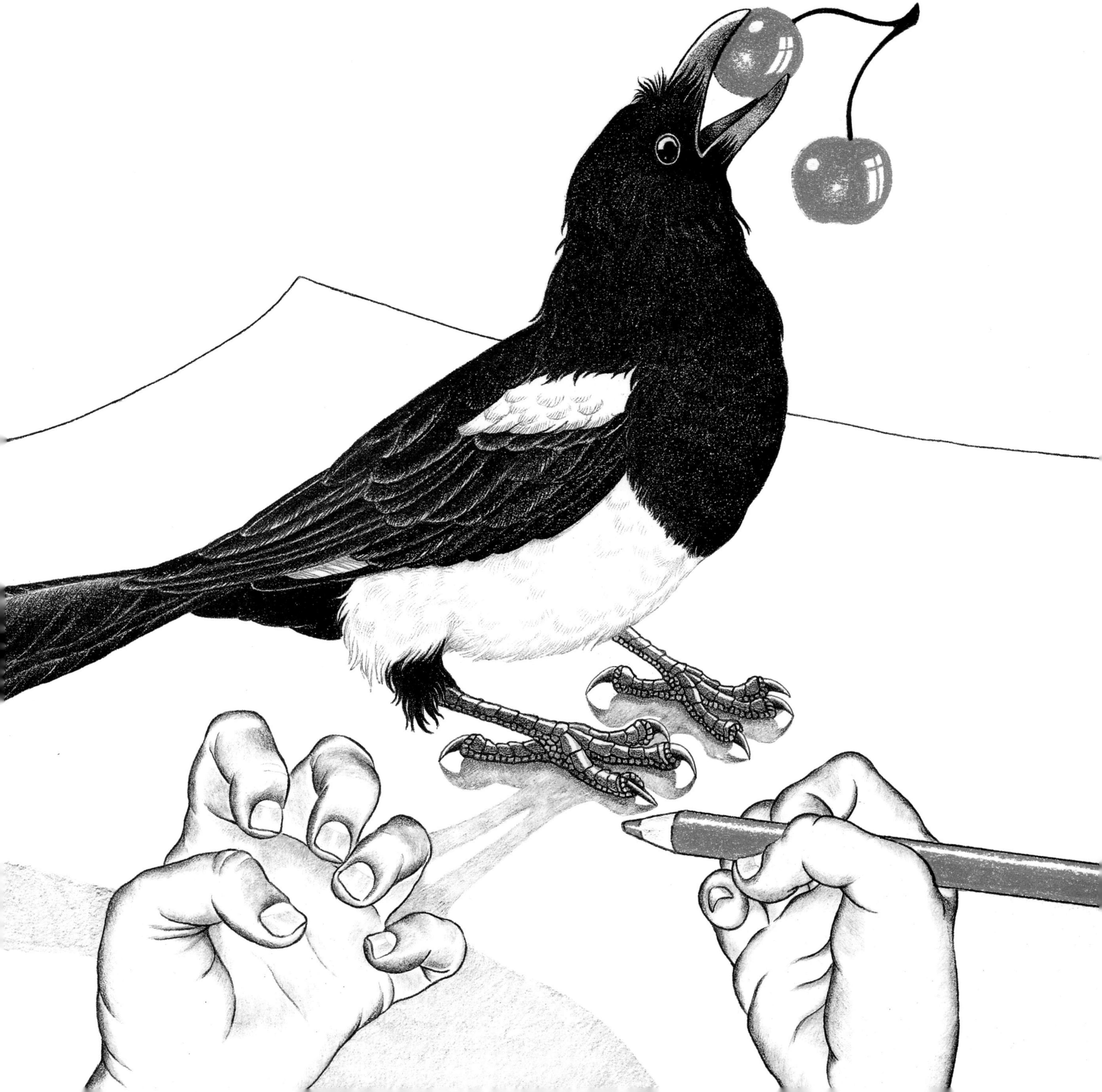

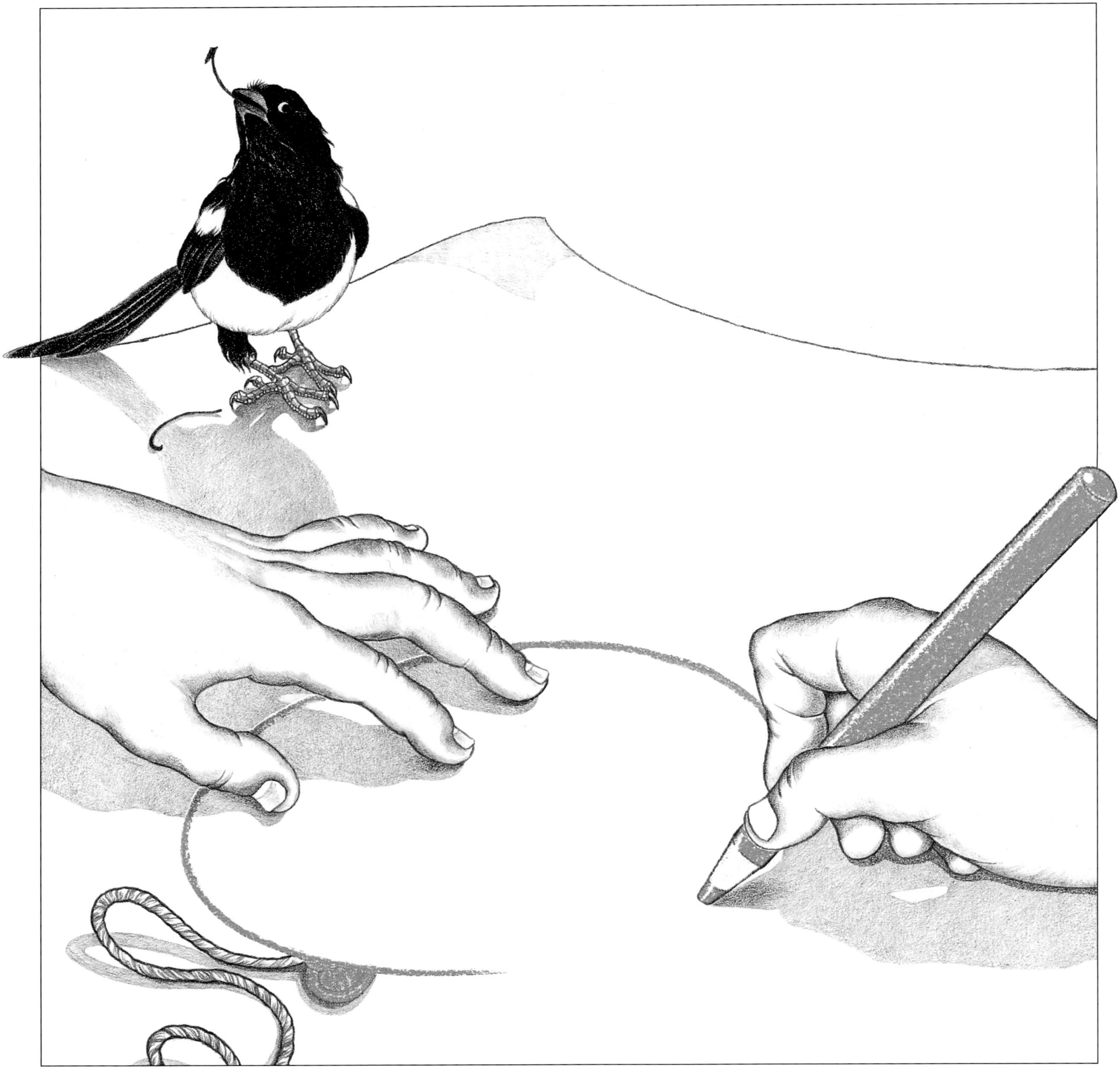

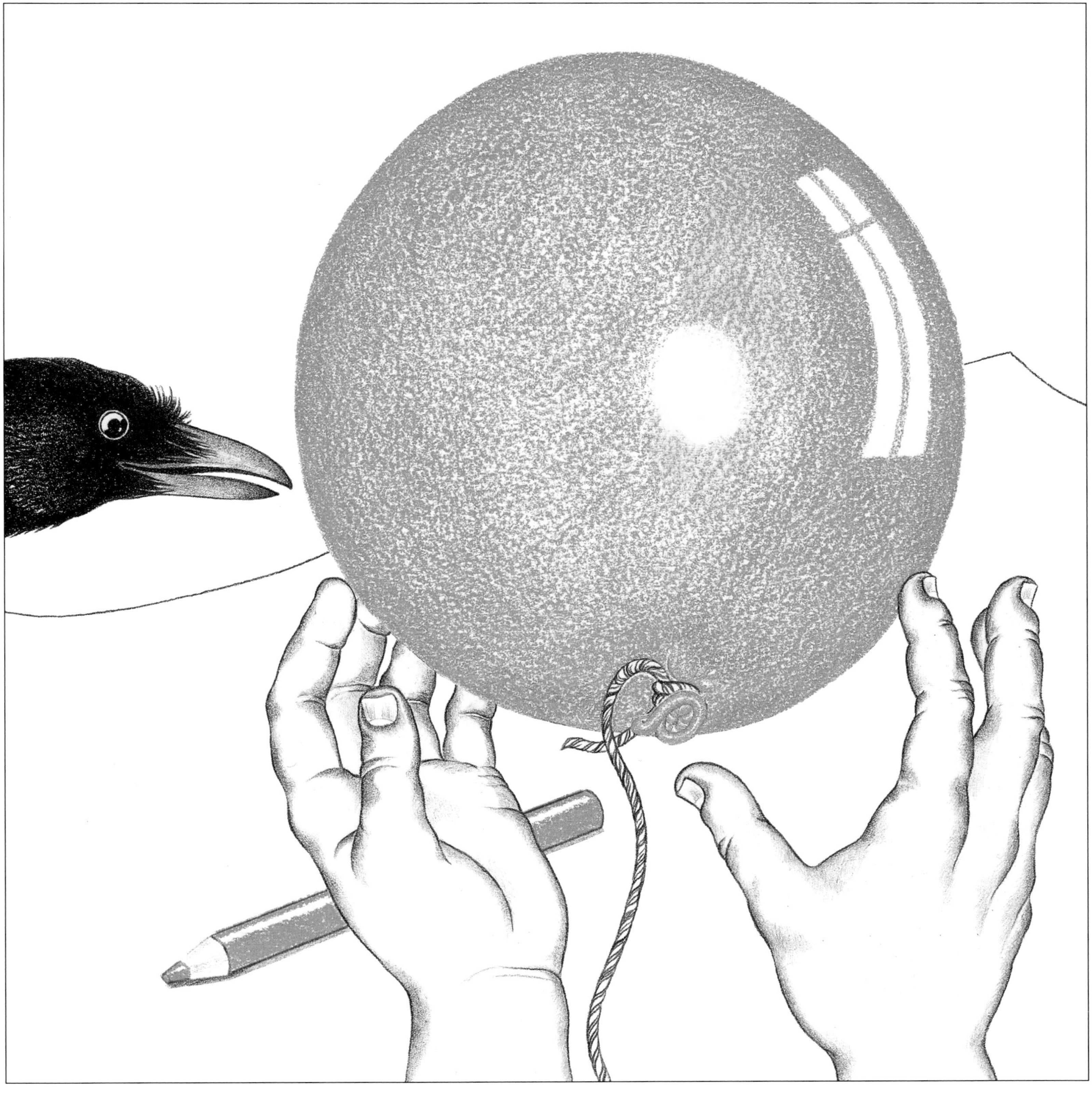

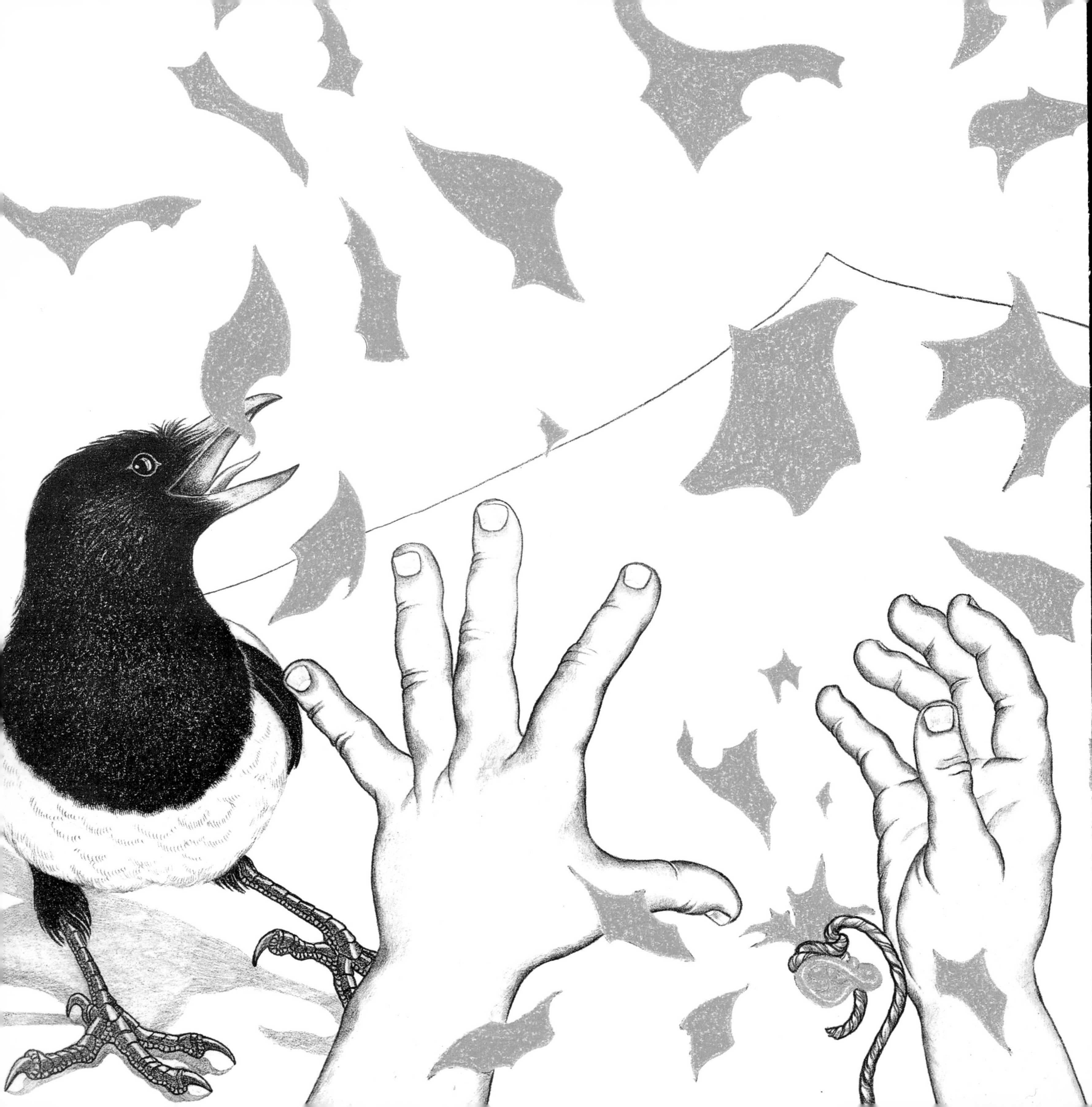

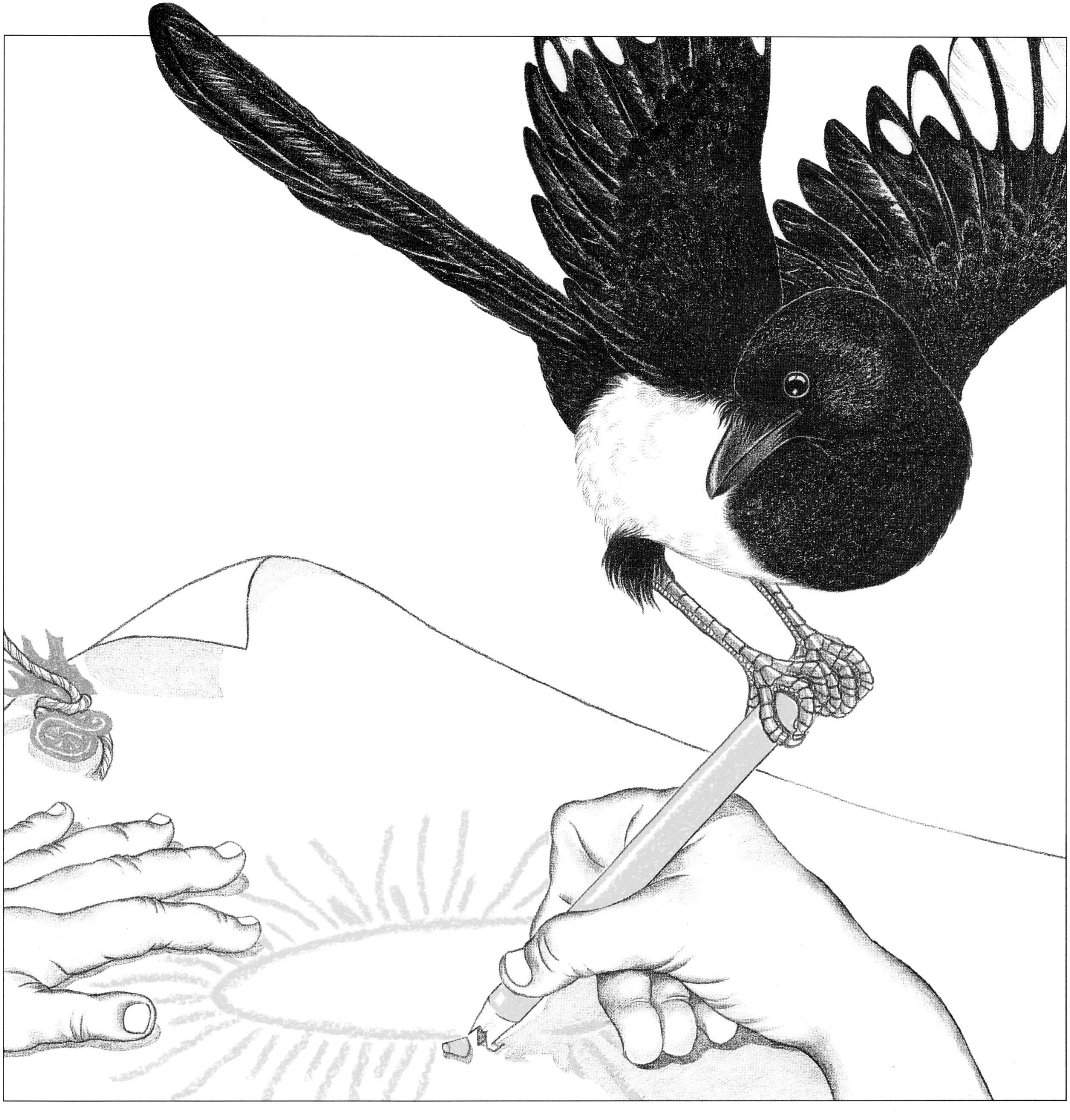

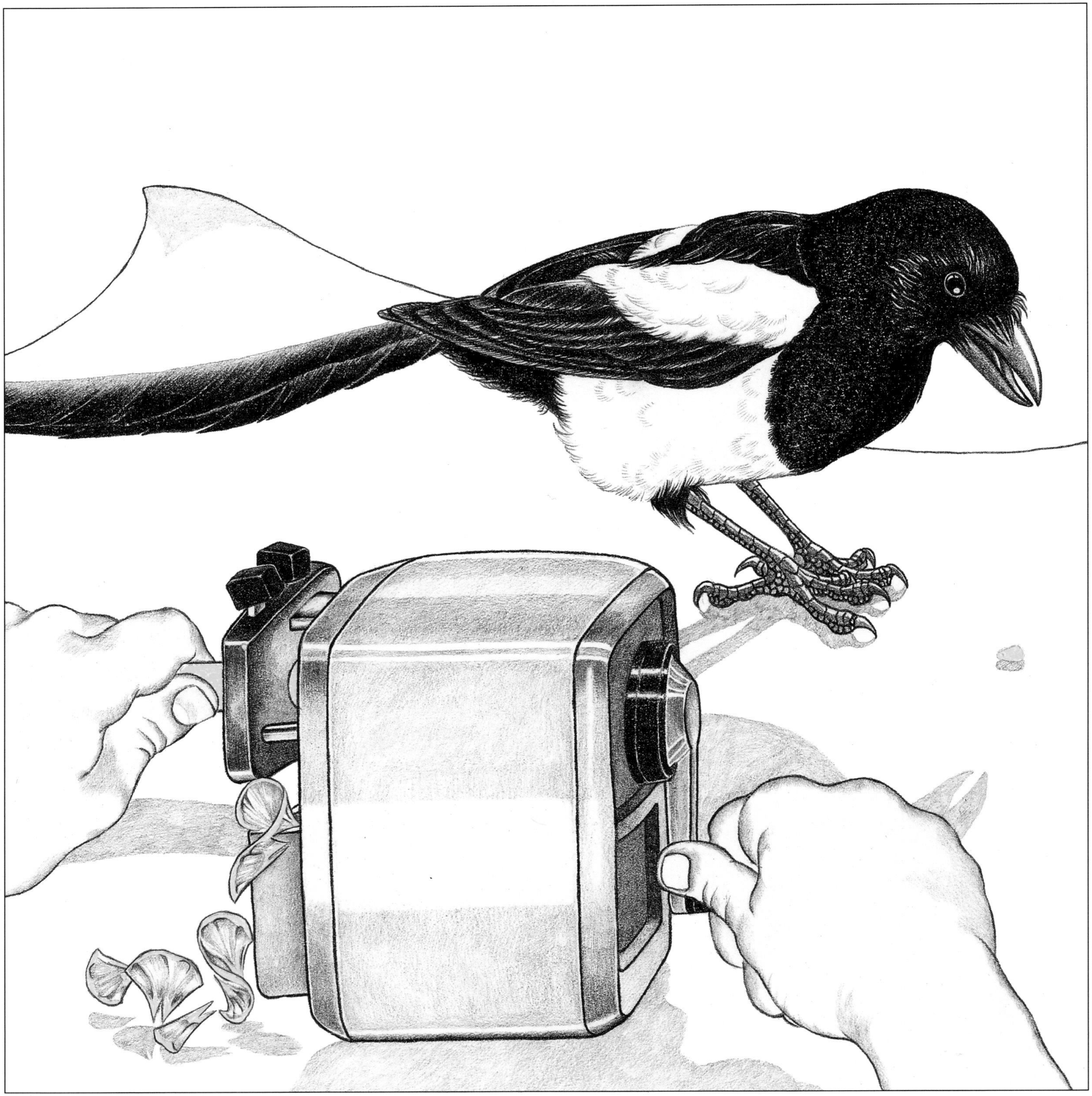

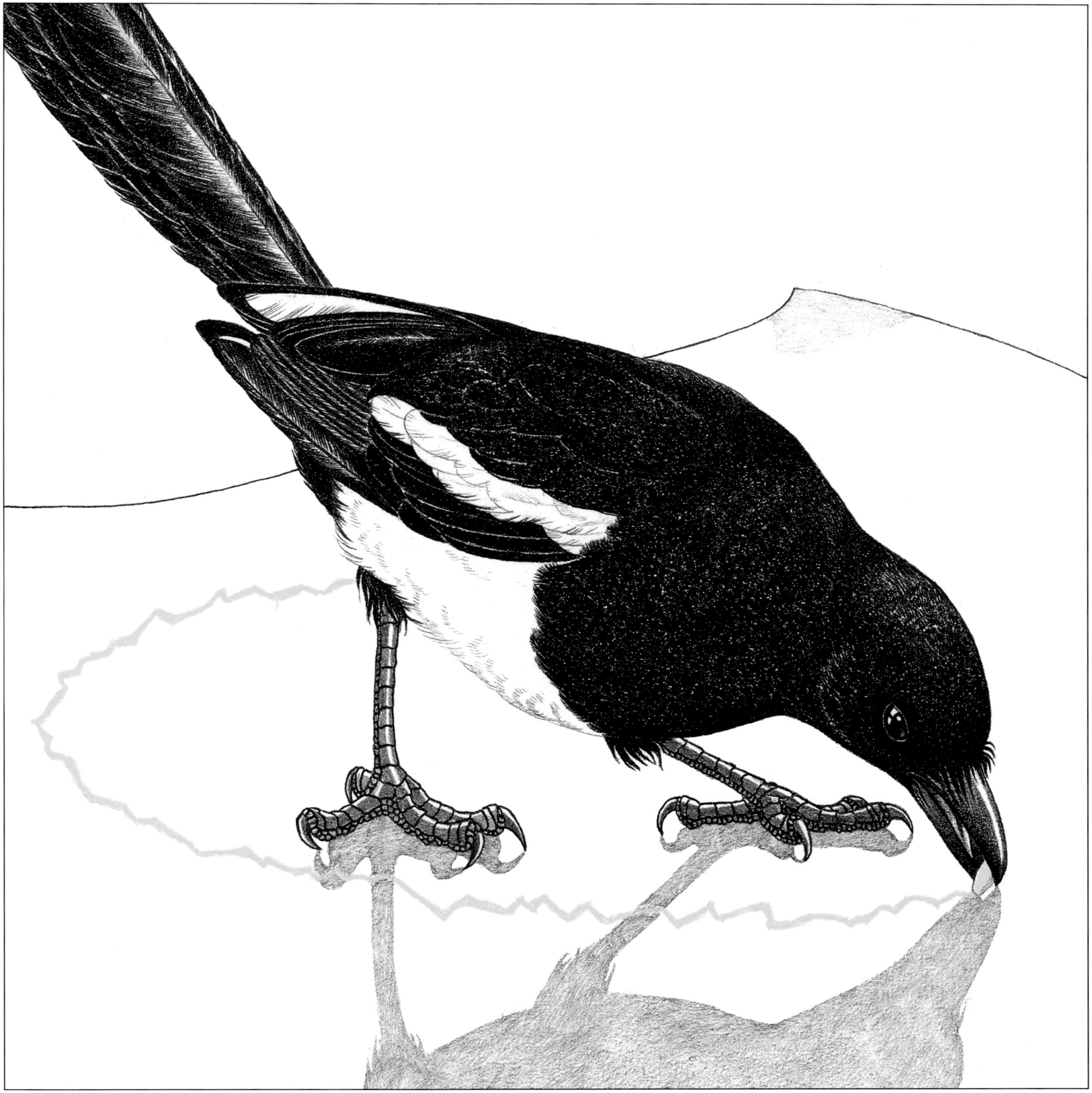

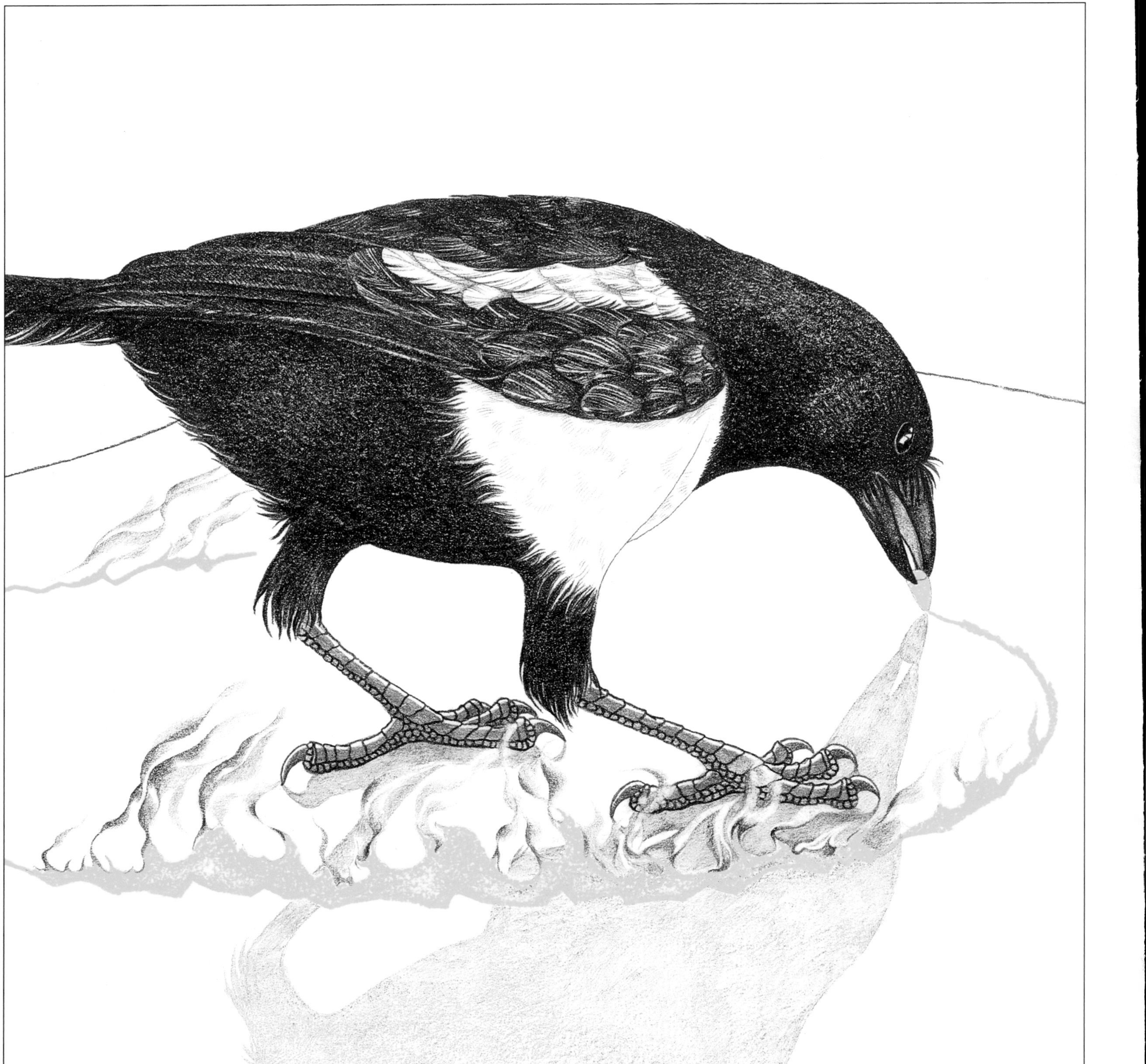

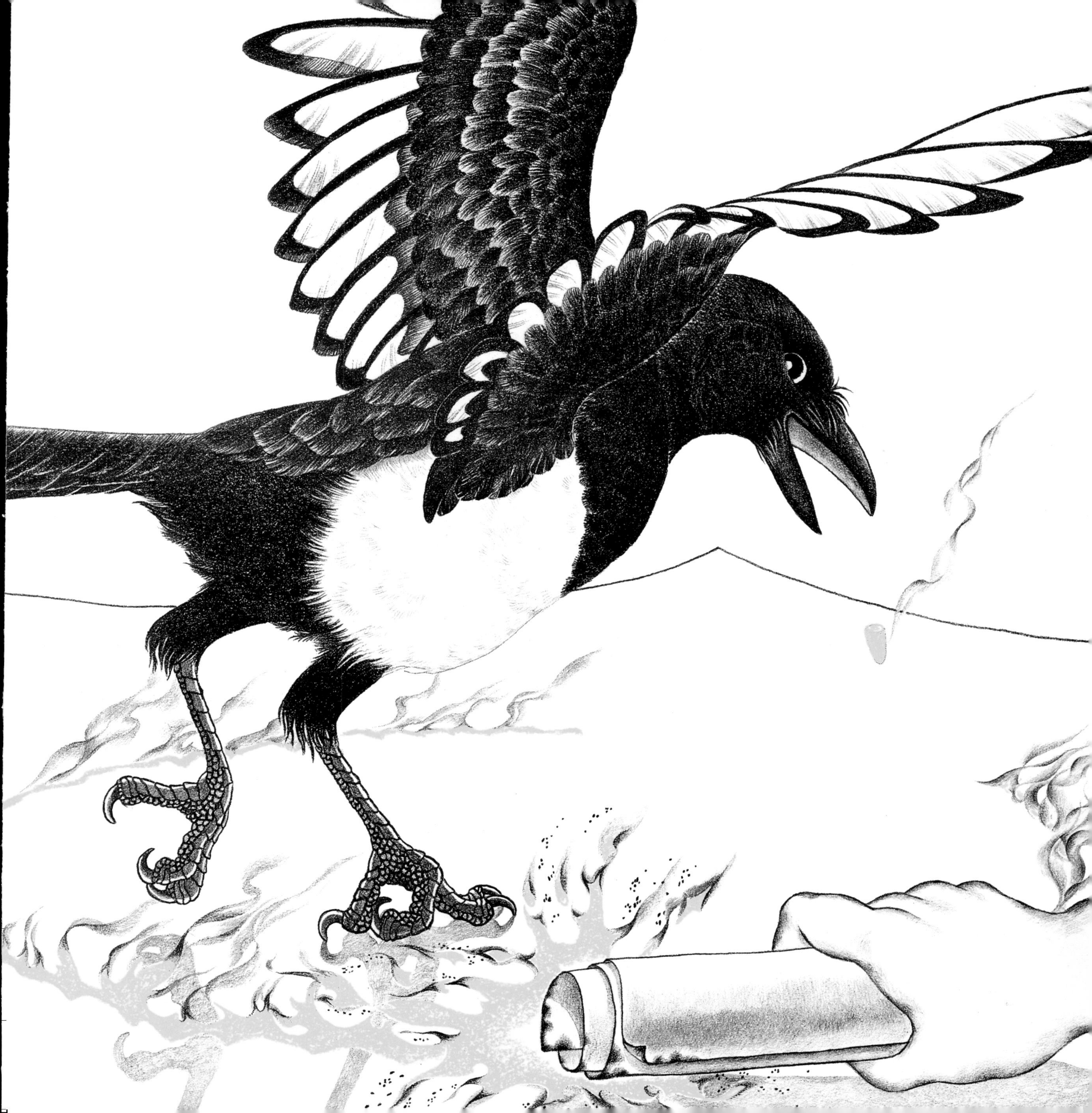

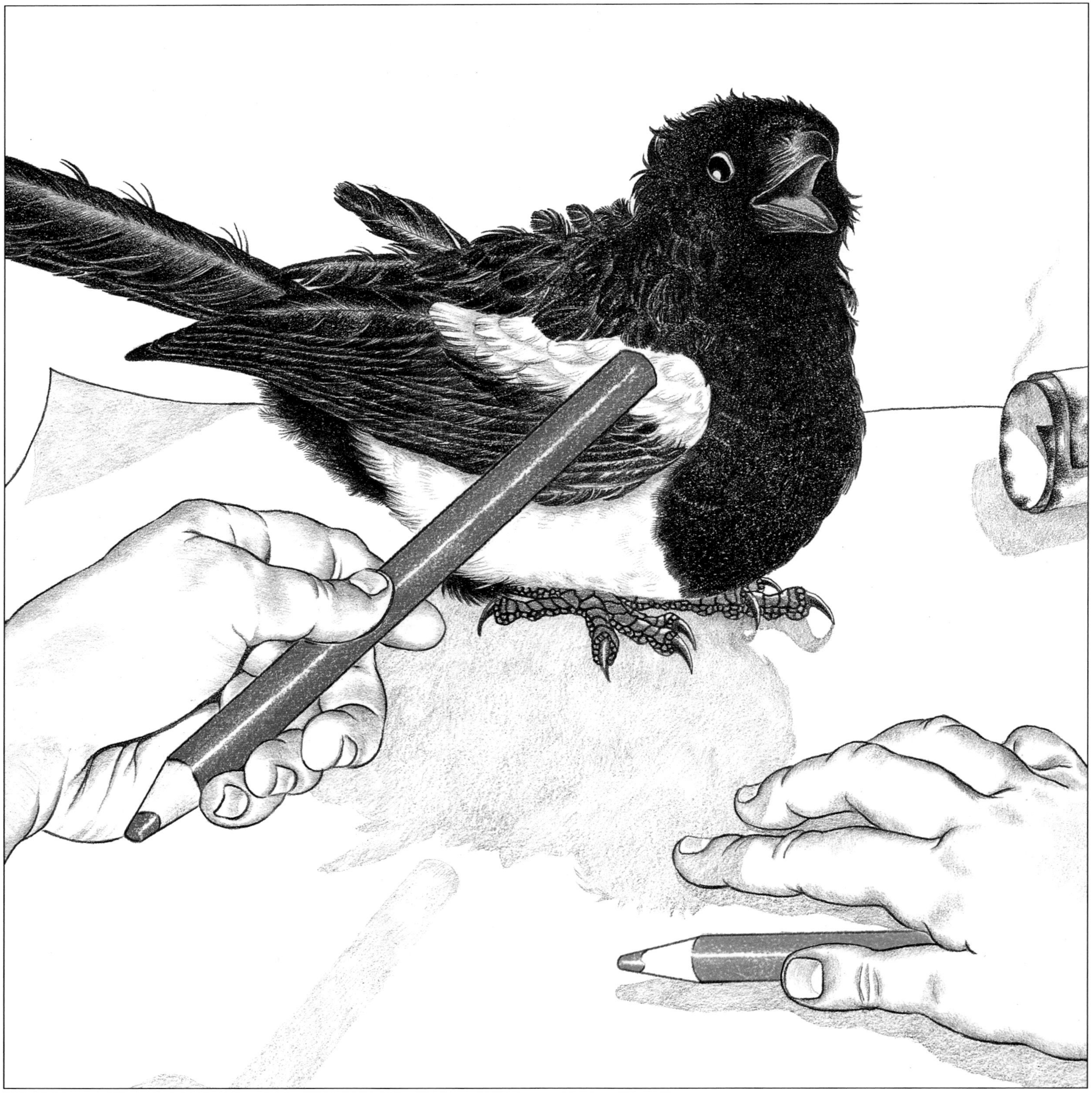

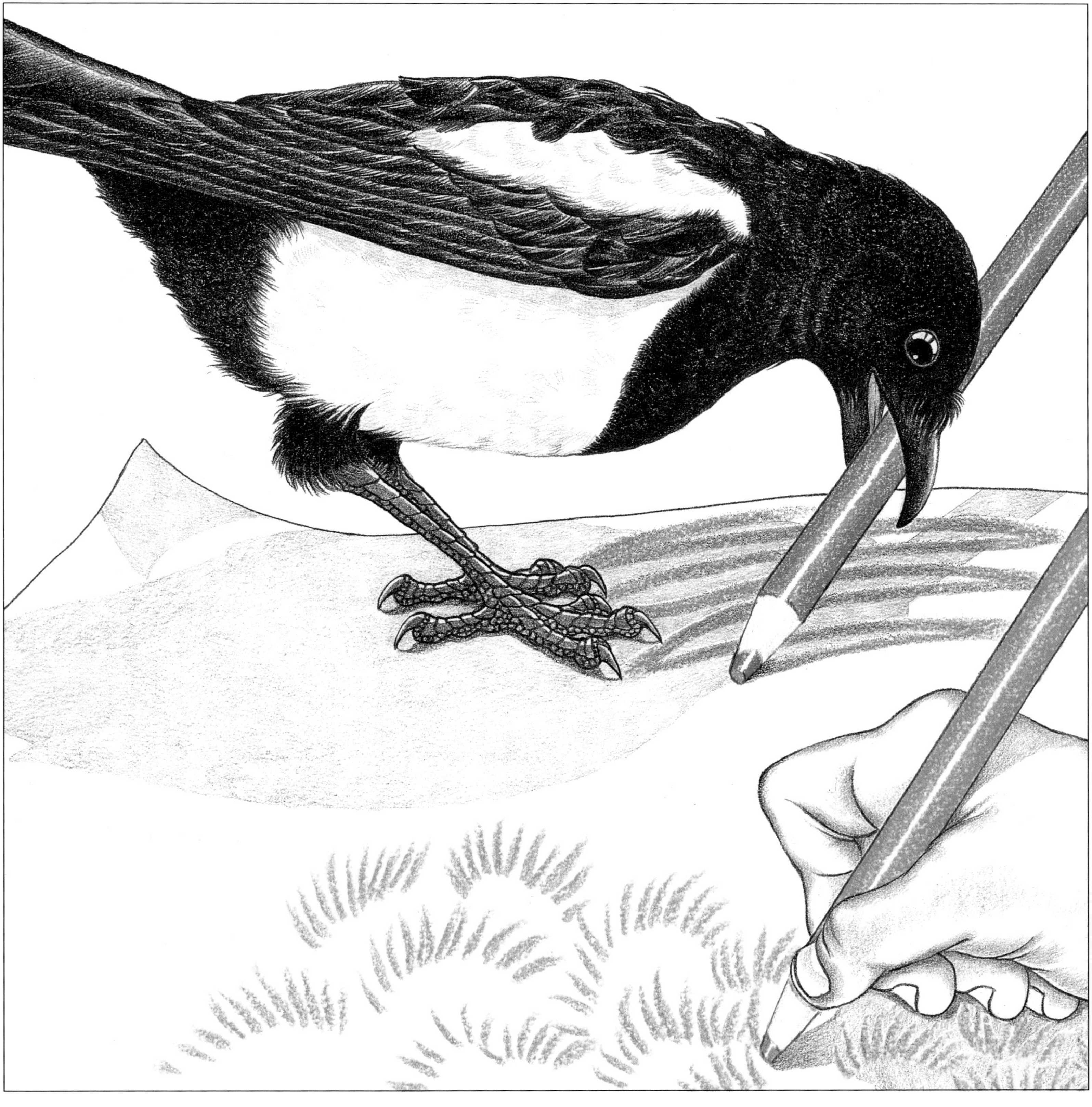

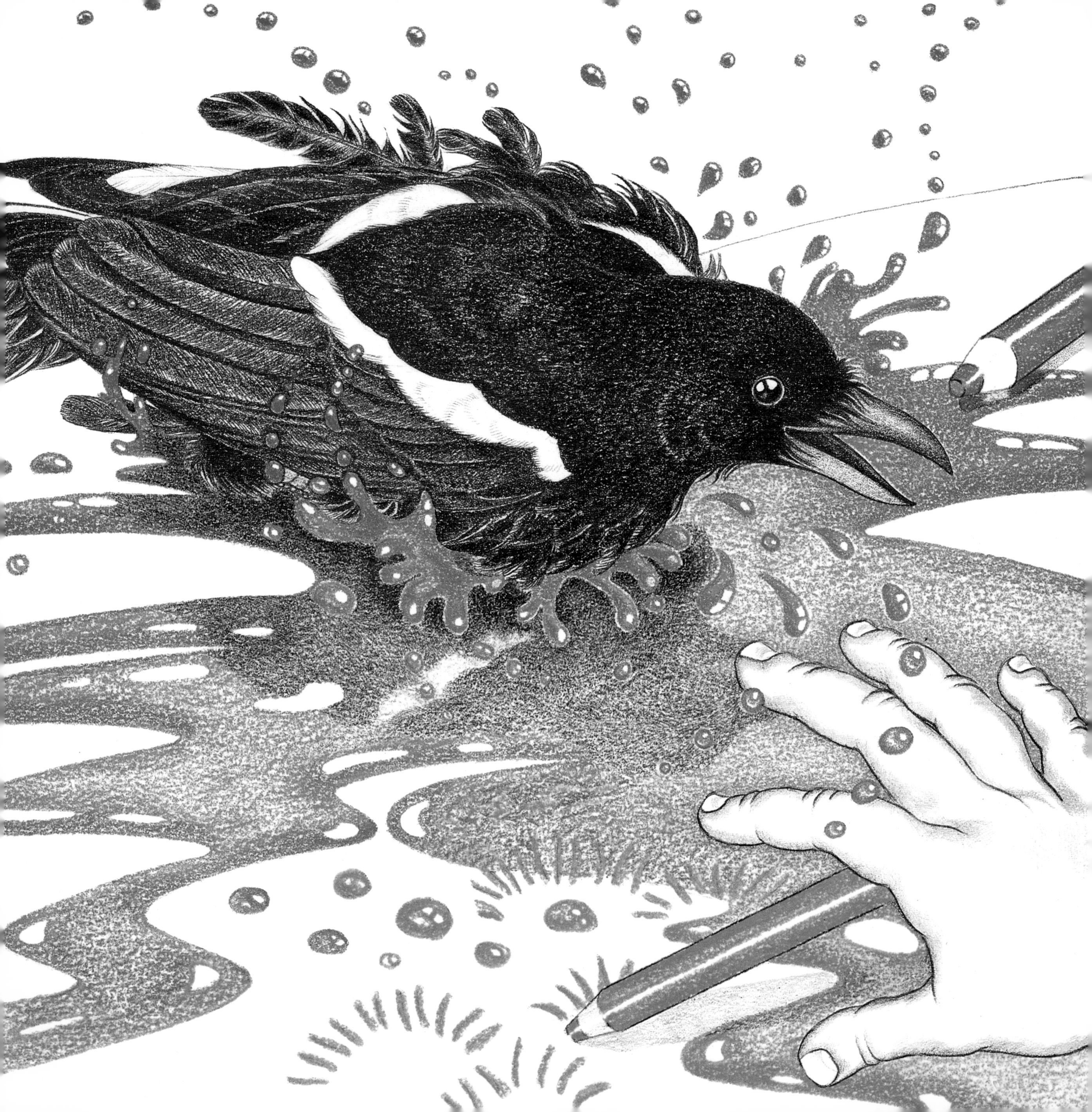

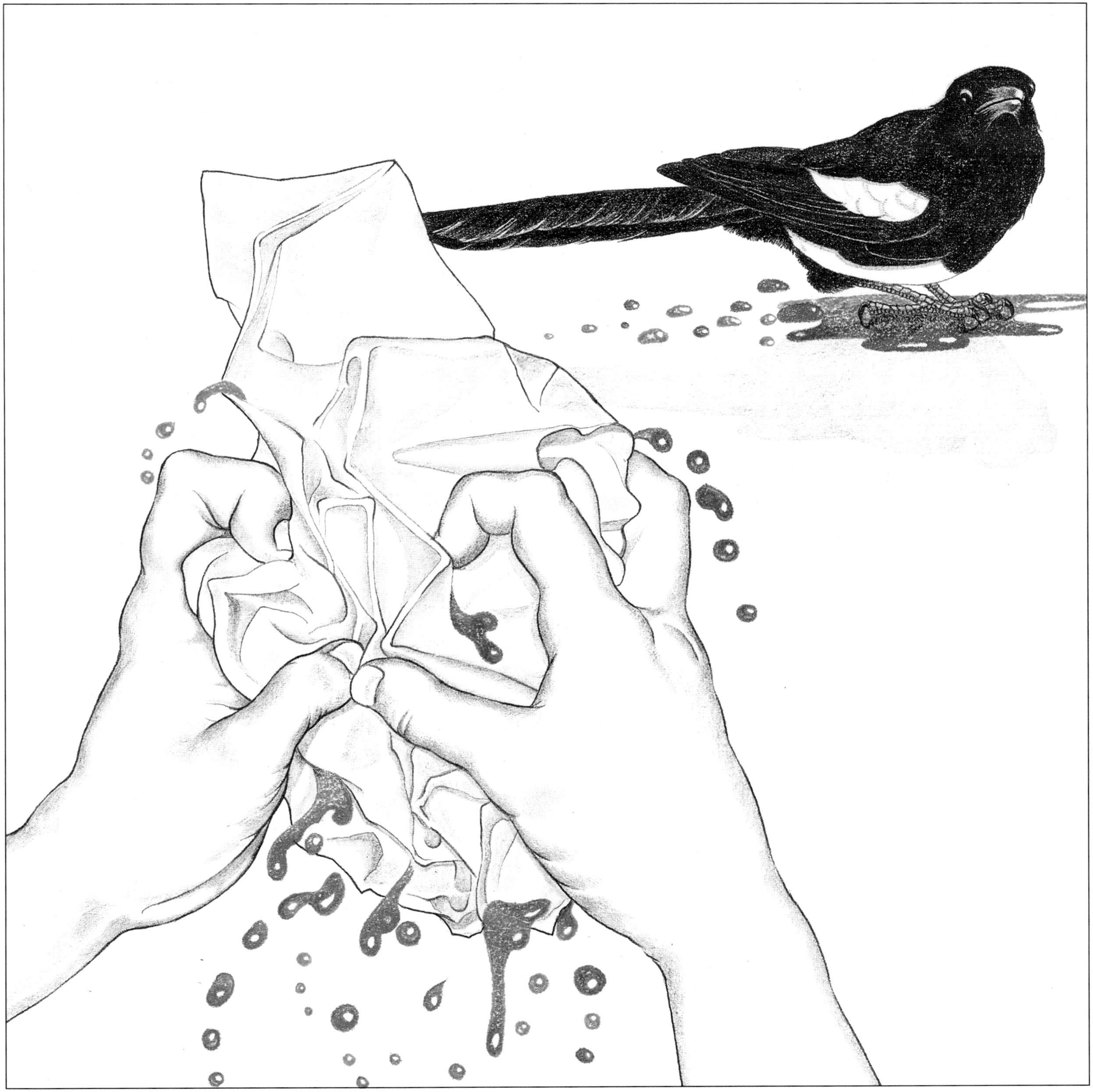

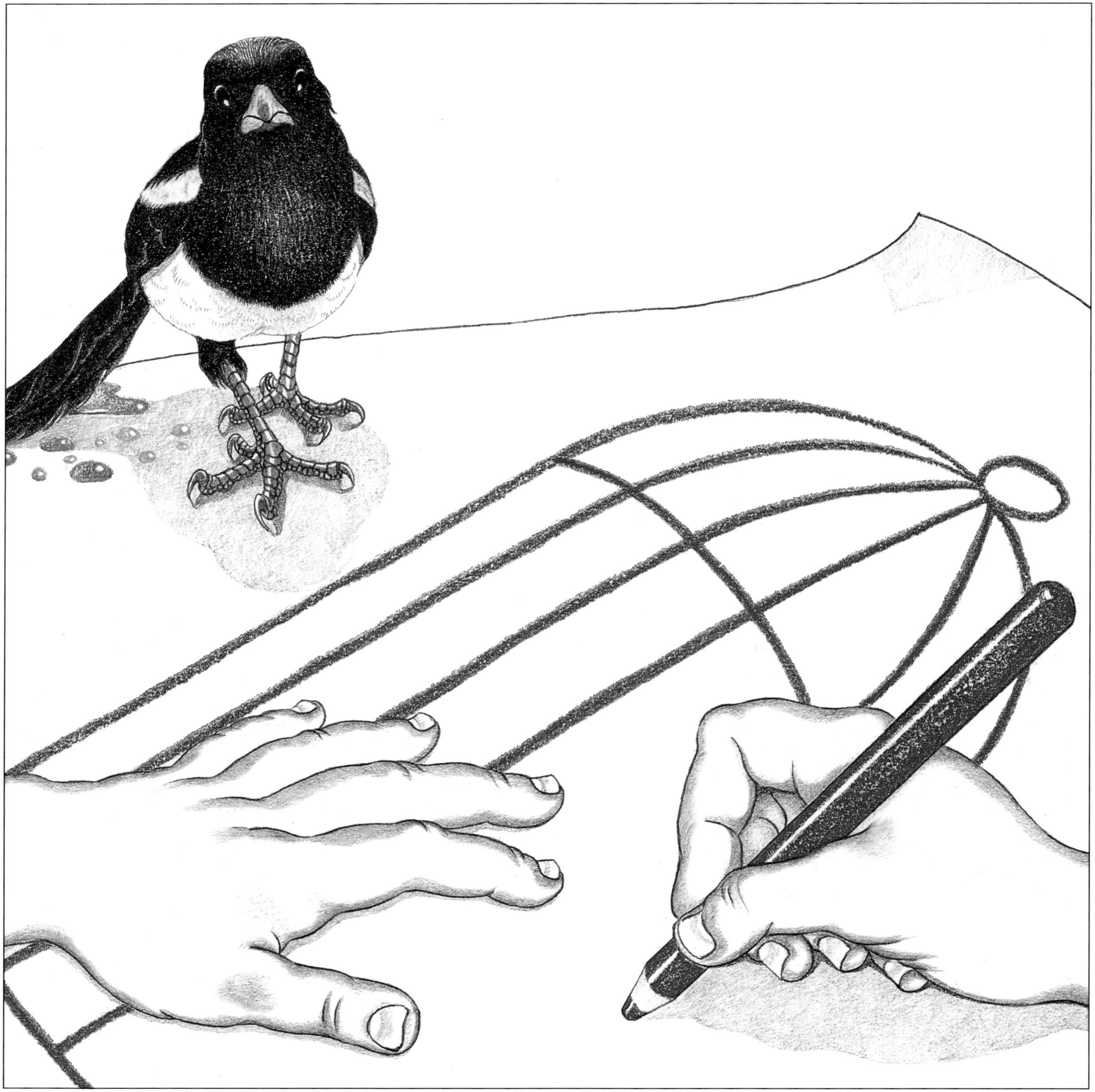

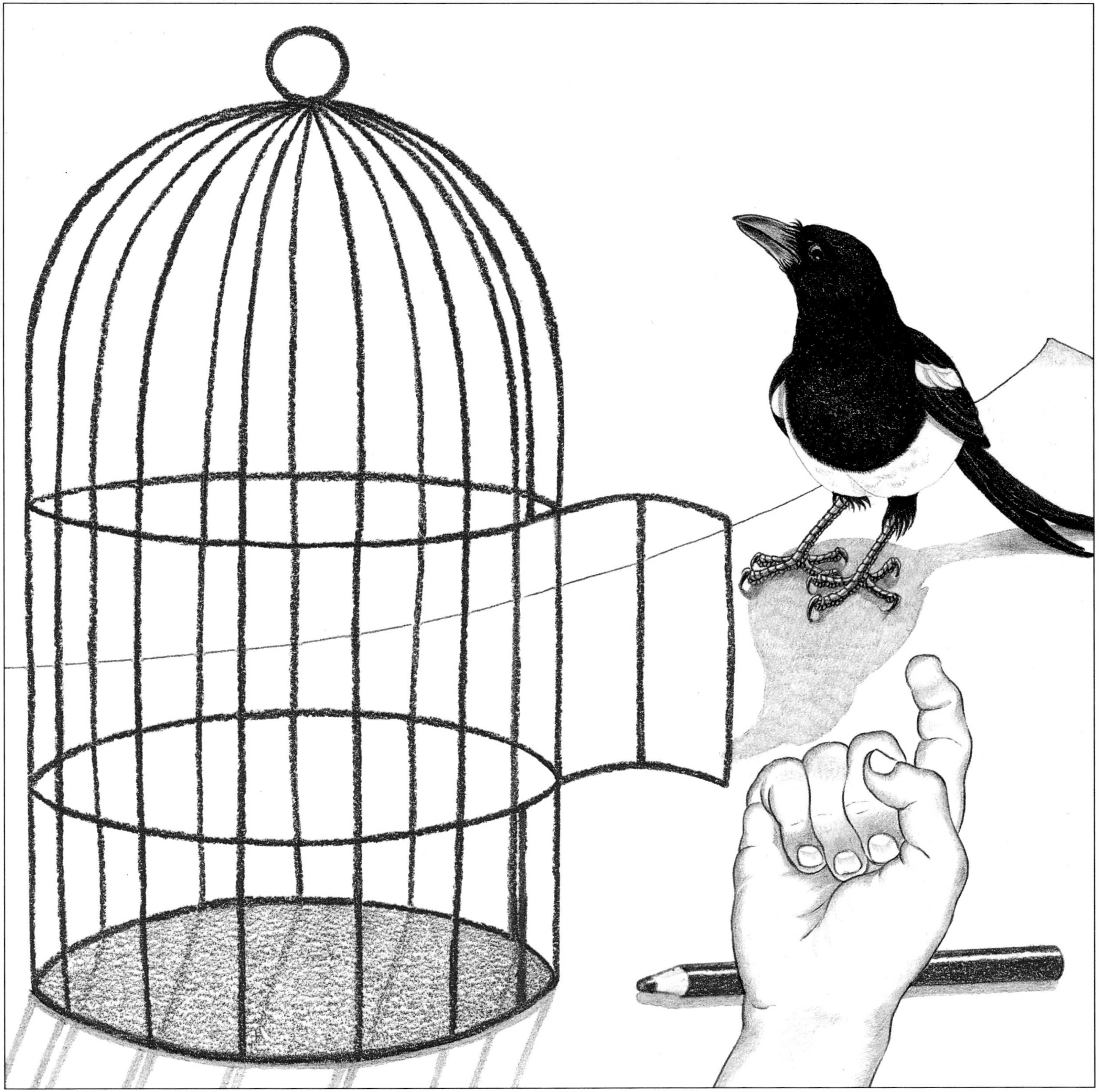

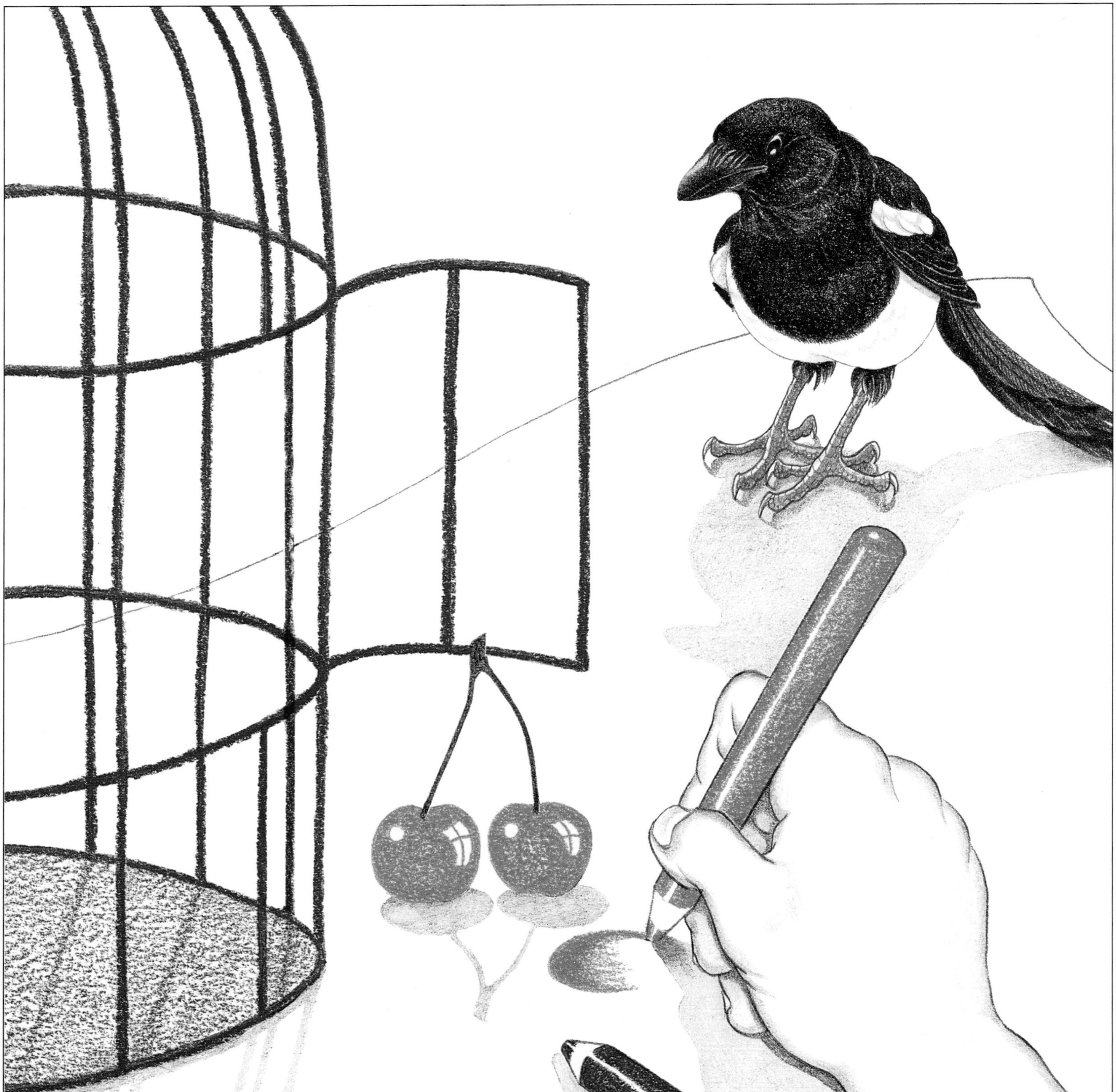

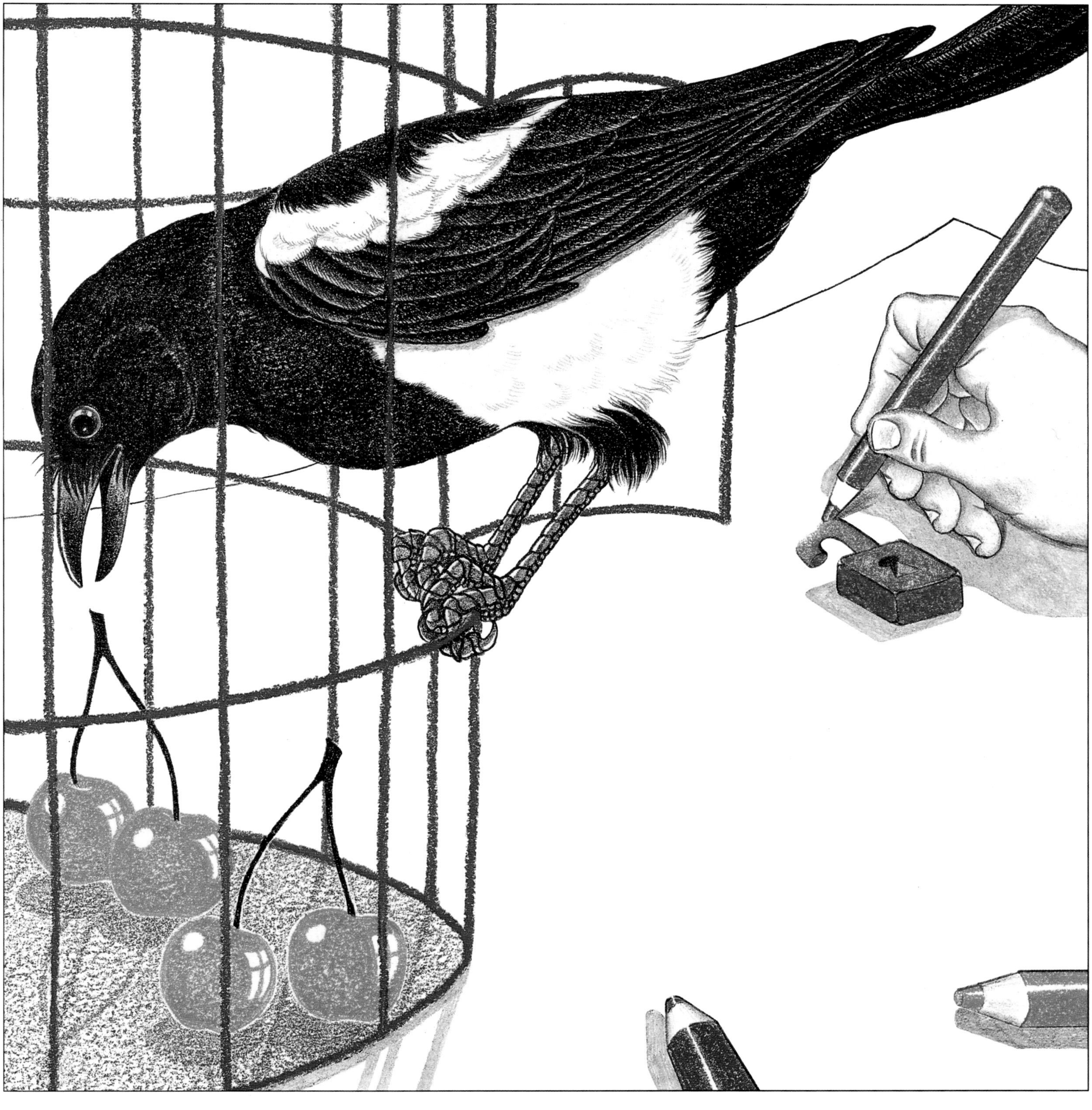

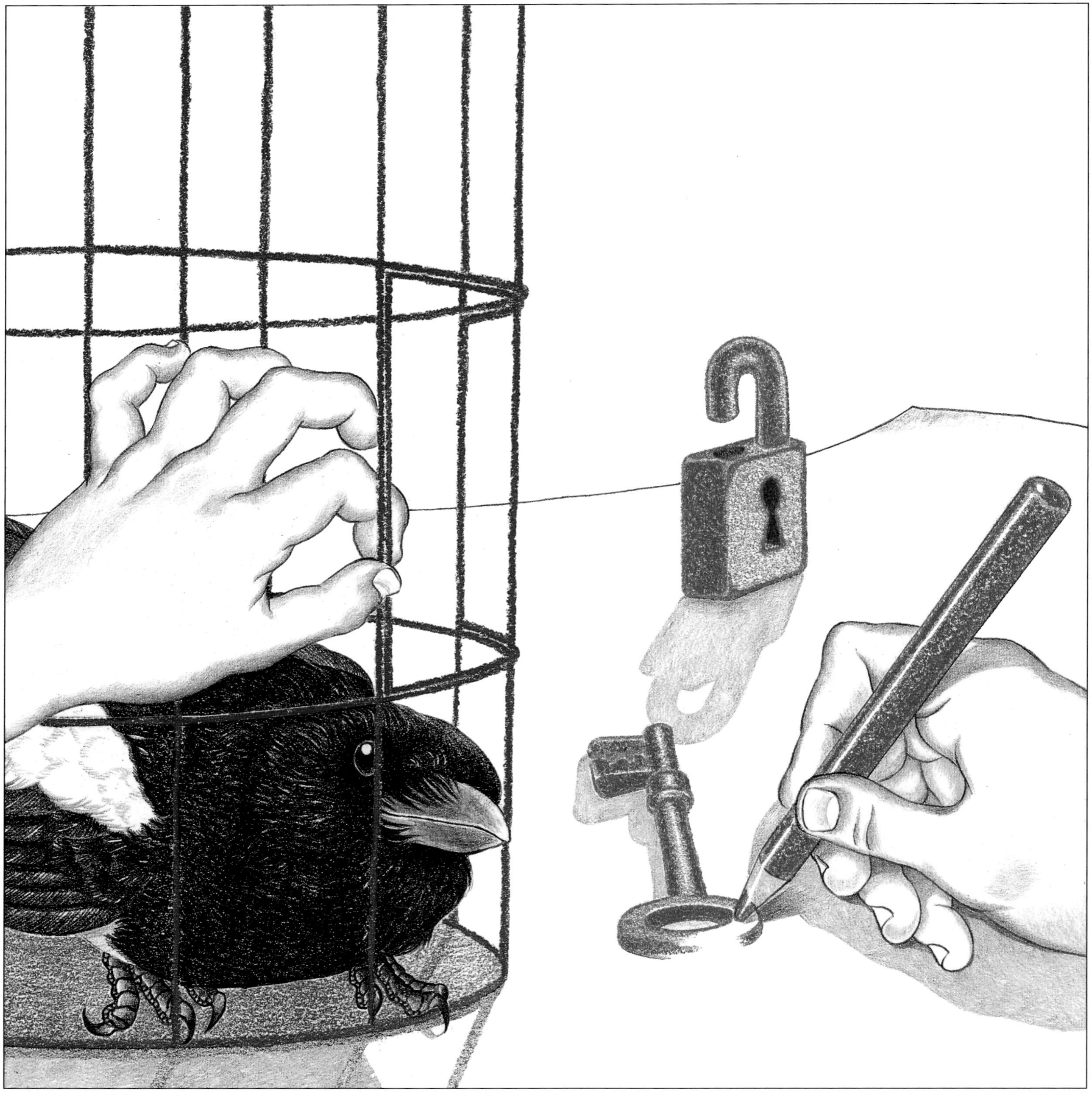

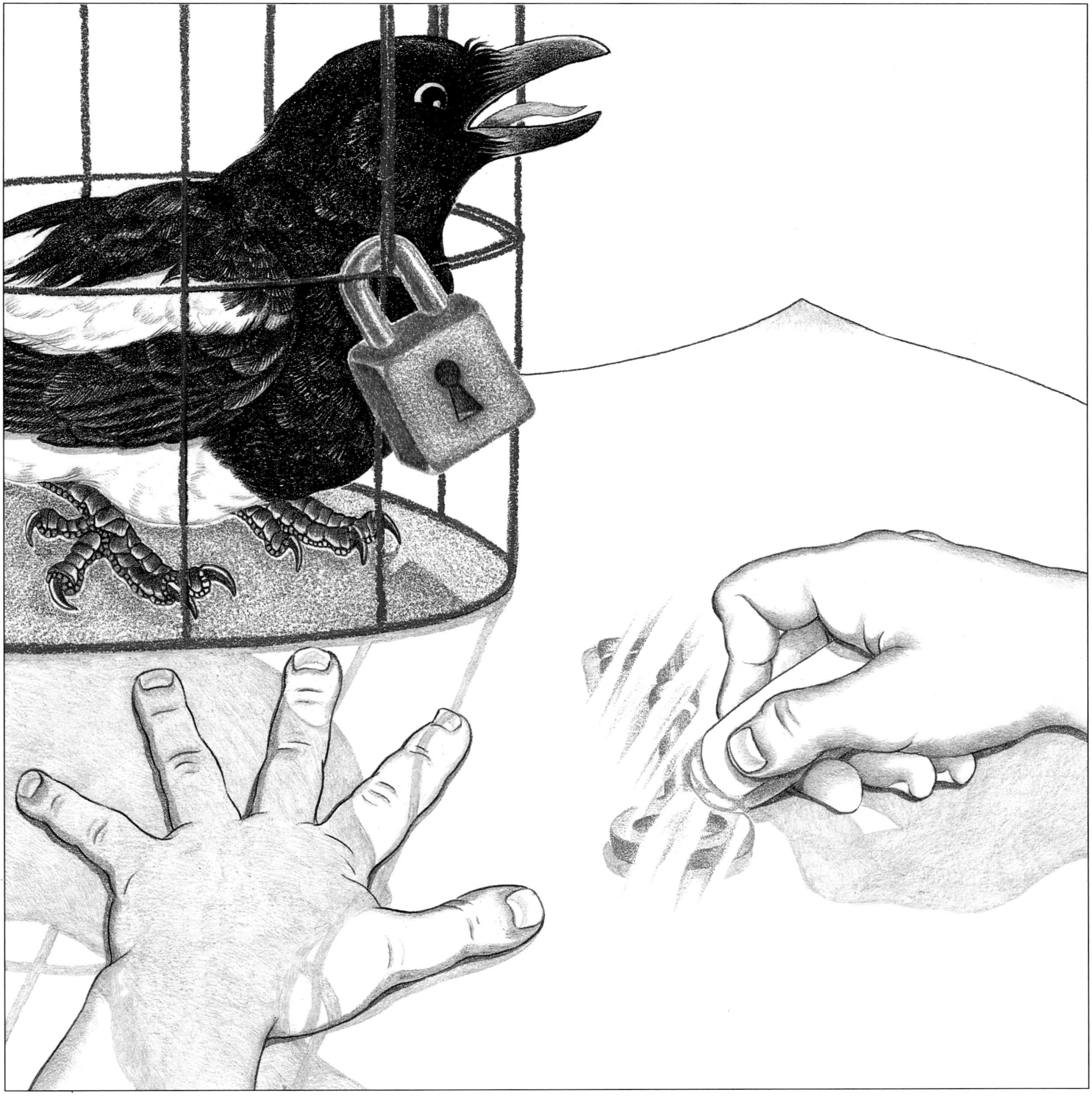

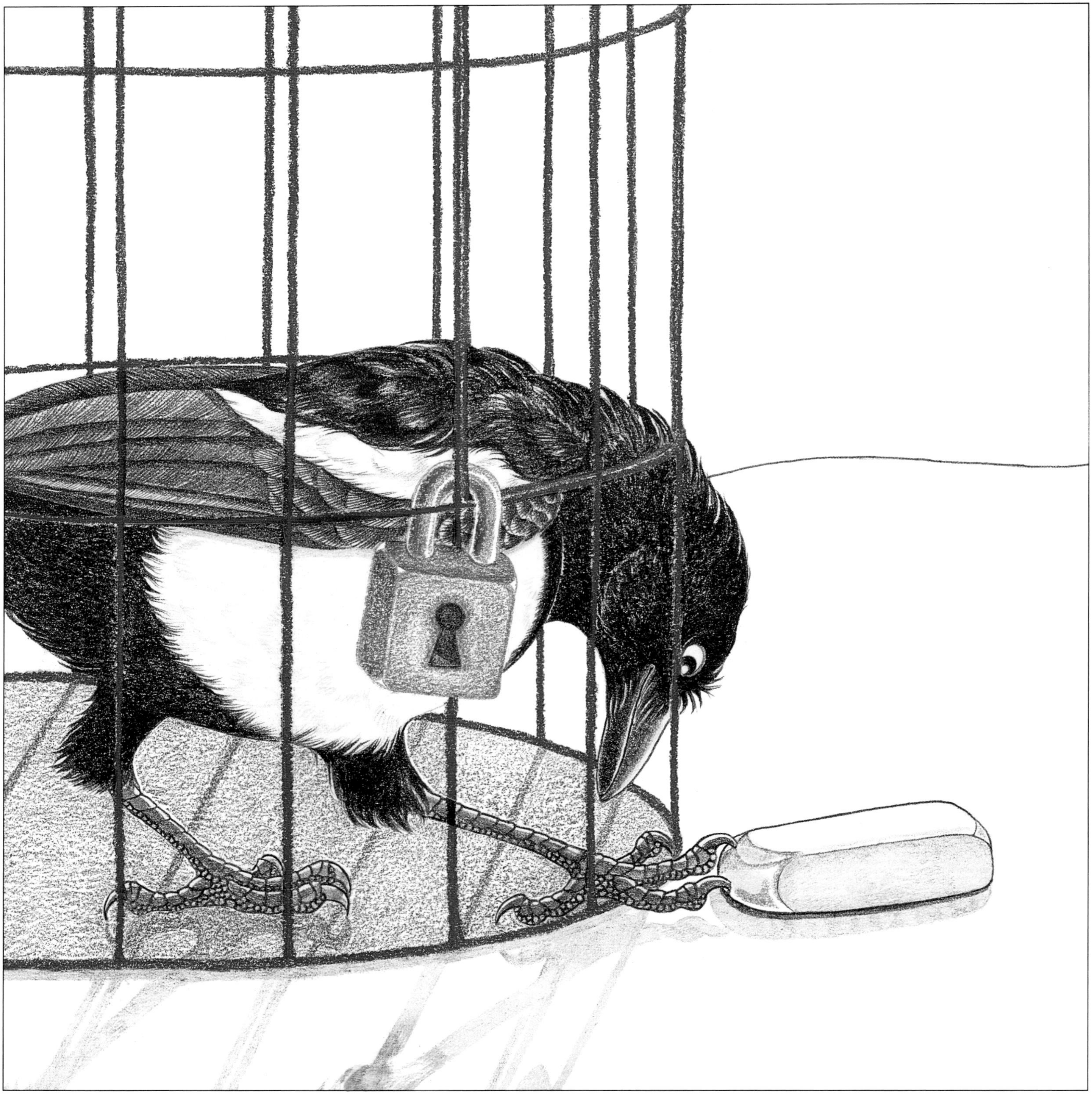

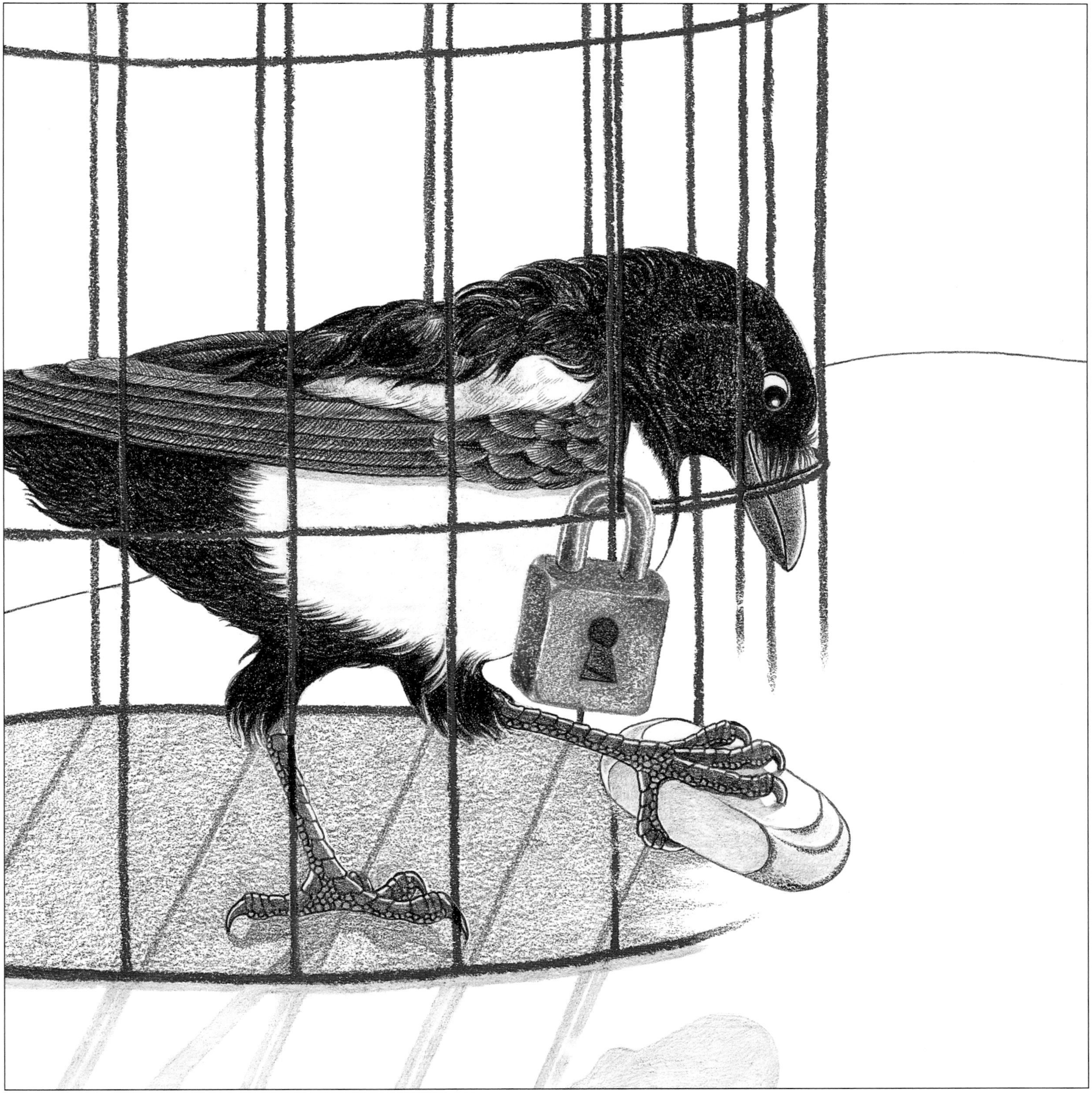

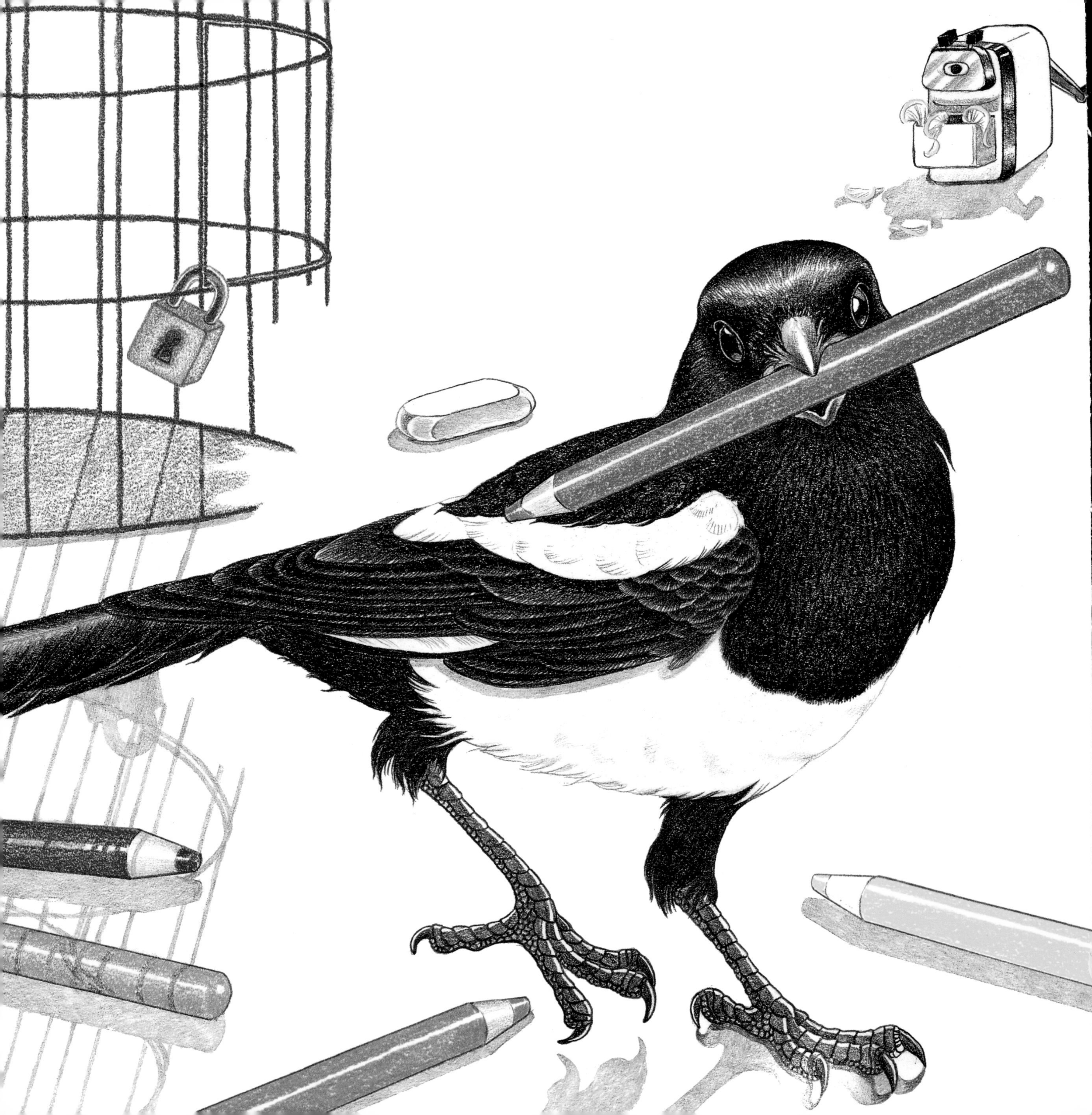

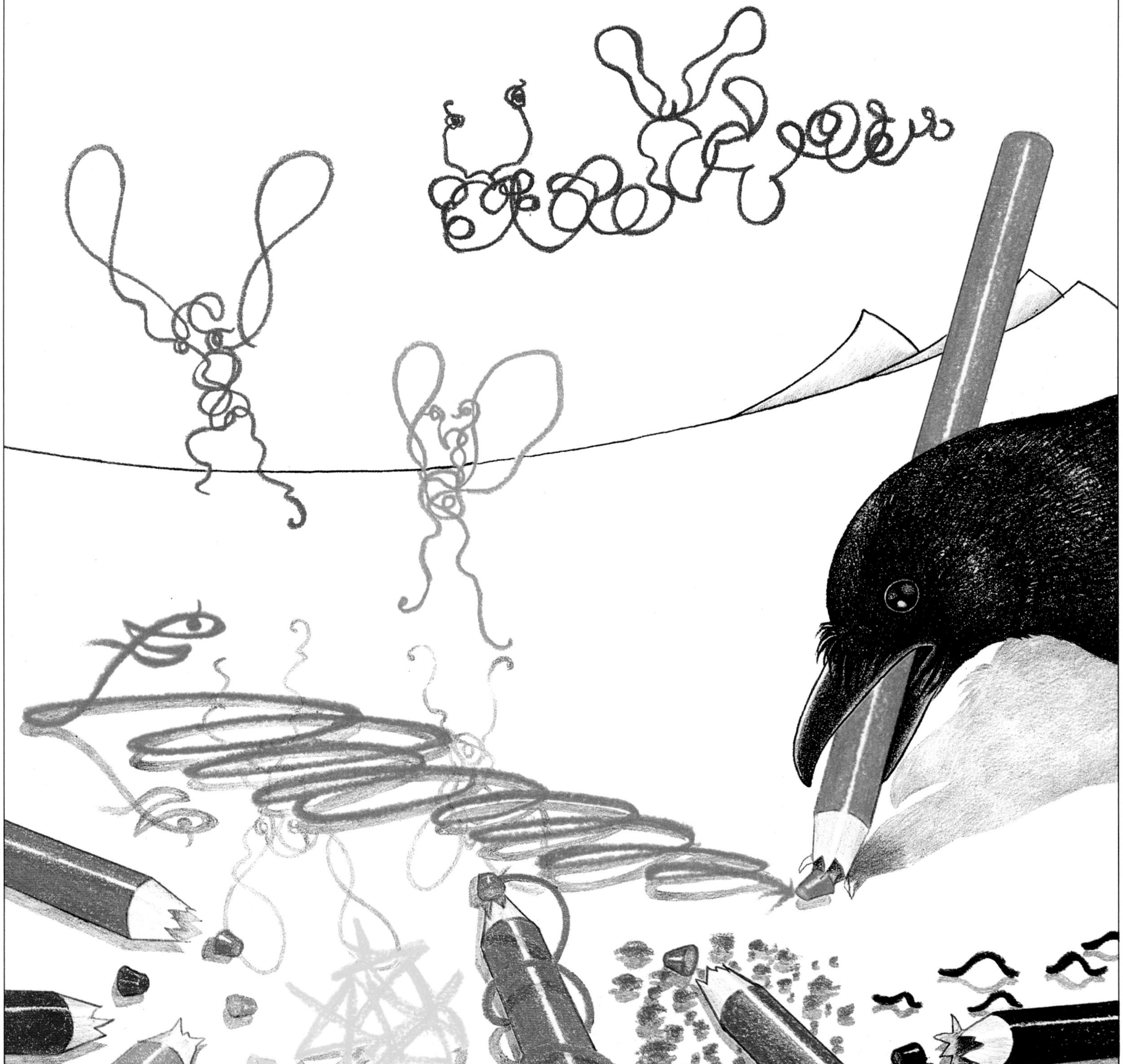

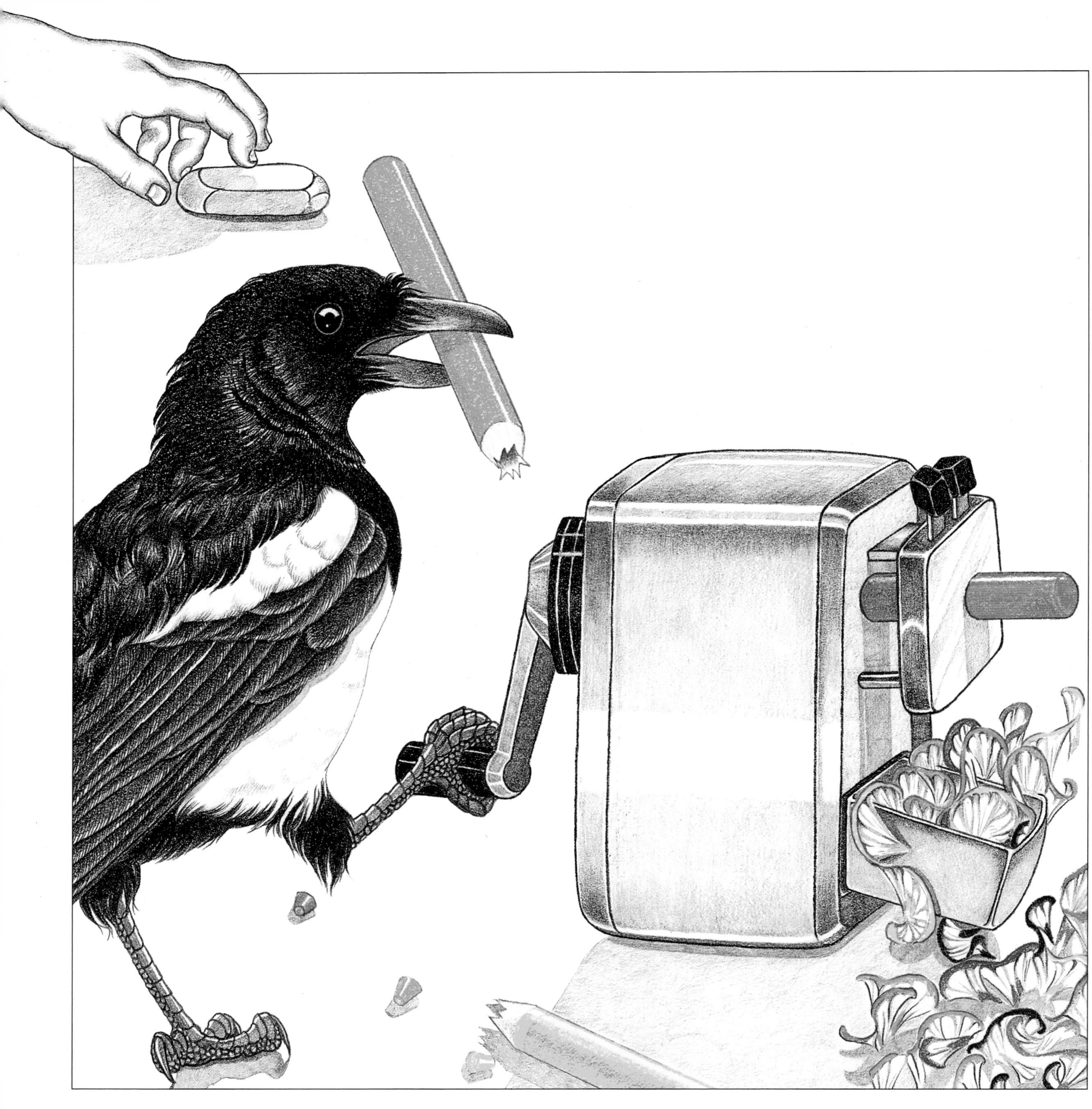

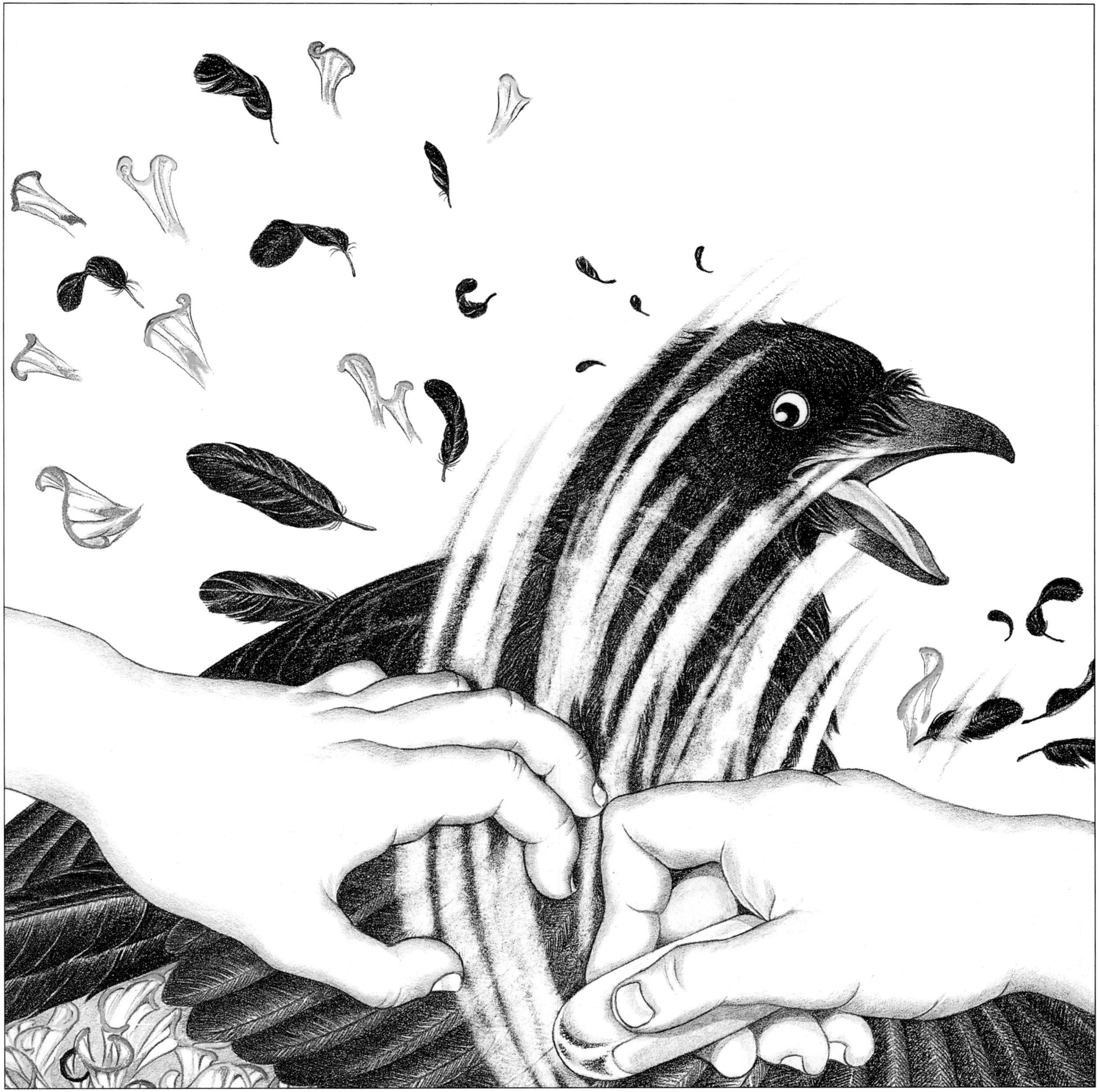

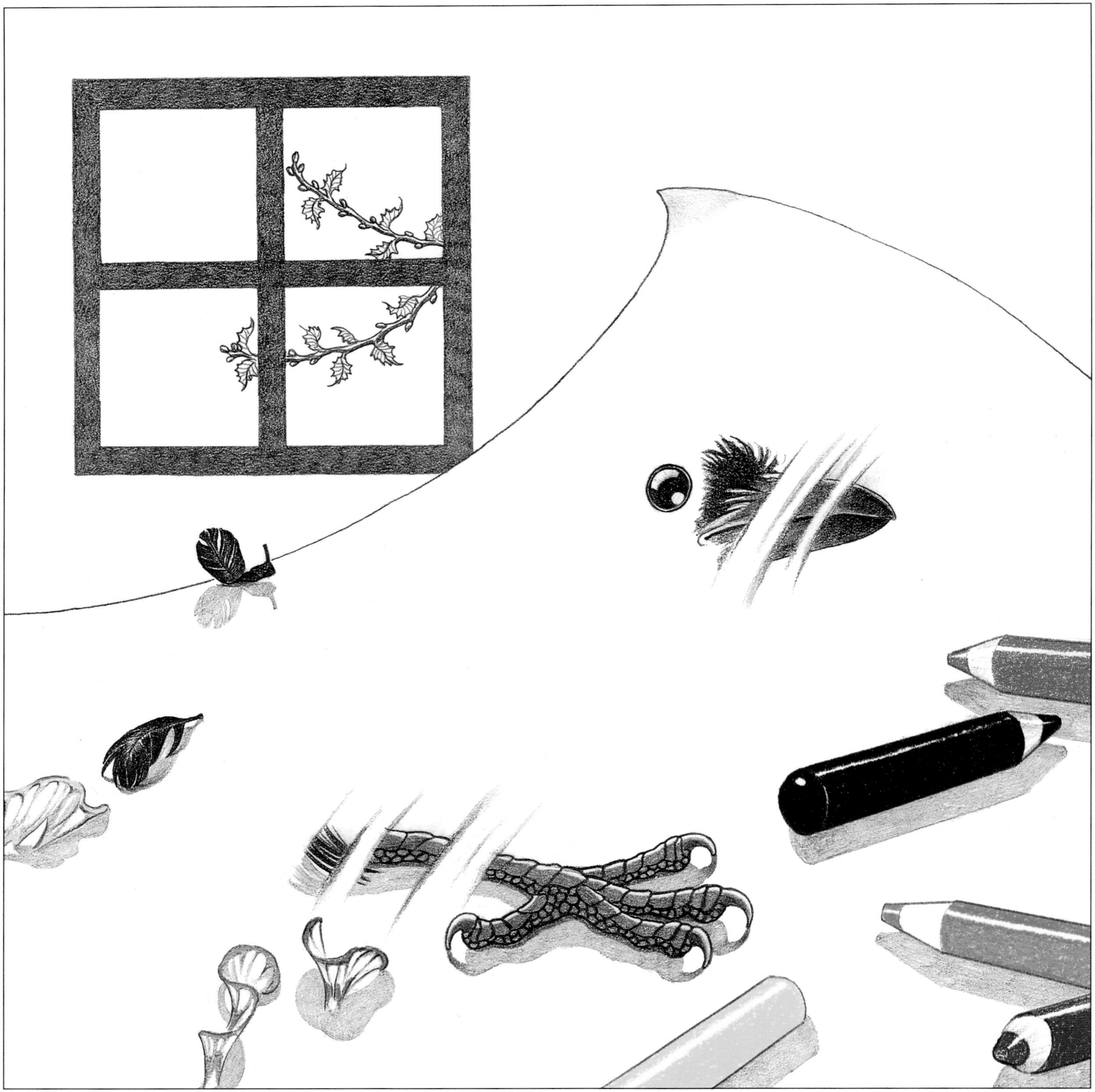

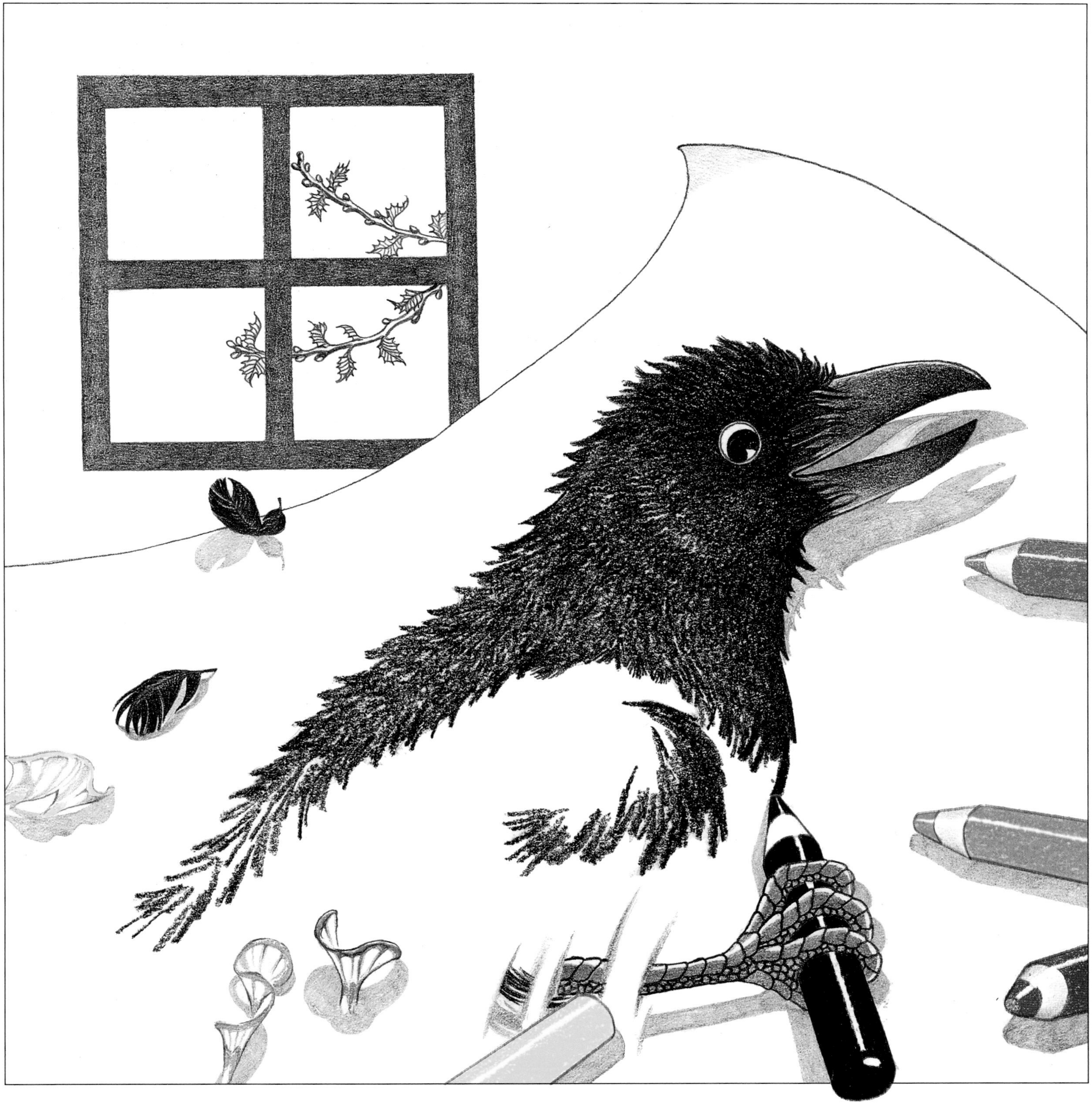

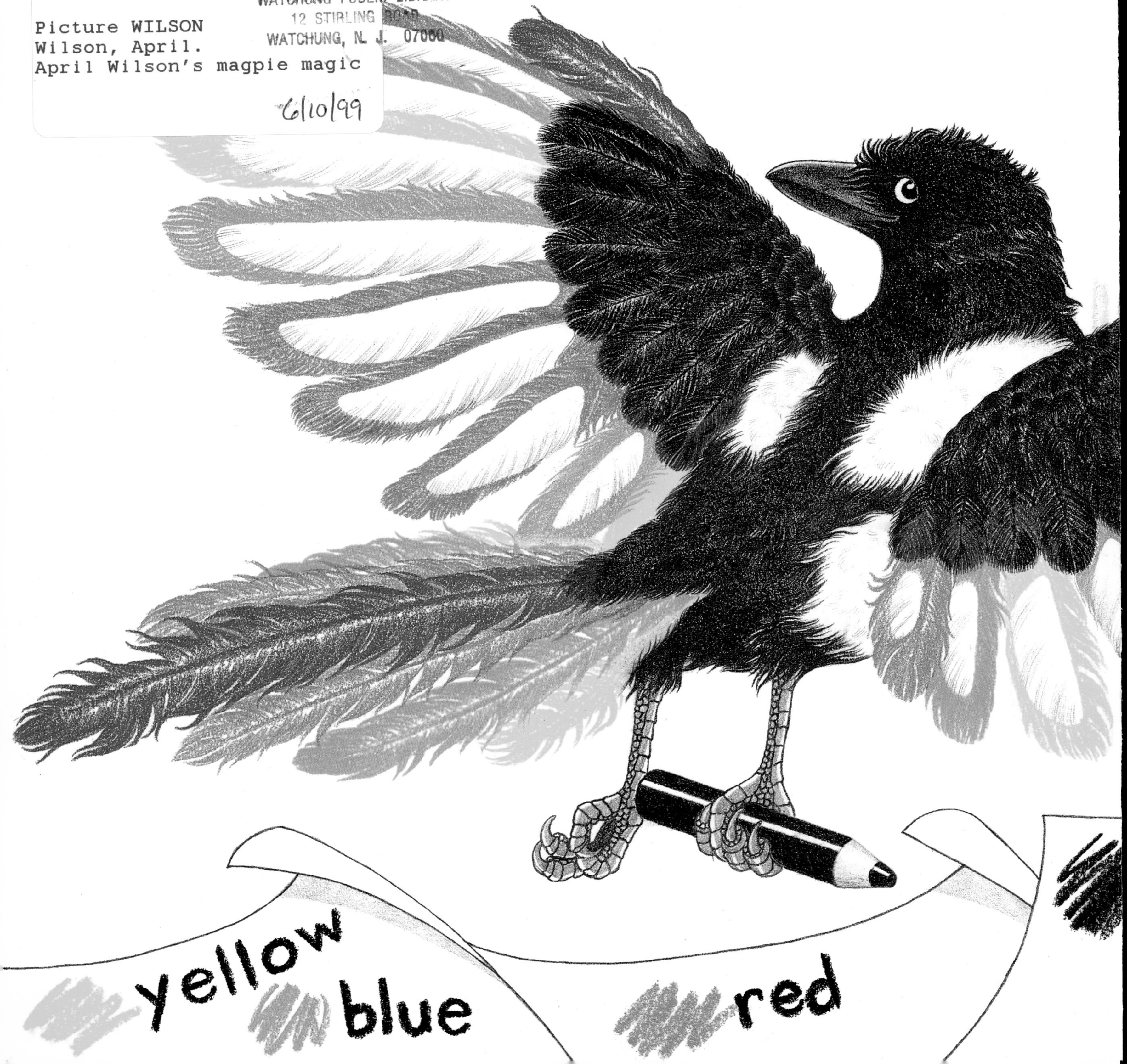
yellow
blue
red